# DARKER DAYS

# THAN USUAL

SUZANNAH DUNN

*British Library Cataloguing in Publication Data*
Dunn, Suzannah
  Darker days than usual. — (Nineties)
  I. Title
  823'.914 [F]

  ISBN 1-85242-172-X

Copyright © 1990 by Suzannah Dunn
First published 1990 by
Serpent's Tail, 4 Blackstock Mews, London N4

Set in 10½/12½ pt. Walbaum by Selectmove Ltd, London
Printed on acid-free paper by
Nørhaven A/S Viborg, Denmark

For Jo, and Greg, for everything;
and for Julia and Steve

Thanks to Graham, Tony and Richard for friendship
and encouragement over the years; and thanks also
for more recent advice and enthusiasm to Denise

# CONTENTS

# DARKER DAYS THAN USUAL

Laura brought that child in with her again today, backing through the swing doors dragging the pushchair as the nine o'clock bell rang. She wheeled the chair across the cloakroom and parked it in the corner by the shoe rack, applying the brake with her foot. Then she bent down and released the child from the straps, hauling her up into her arms and wiping across her nose with a tissue. Then she took her to the infants' class. The pushchair stays in the corner until the end of the day. There is nowhere else for it to go. I watch the kids barge into it on their way to the playground. There is no spare room in the office with both of us here. The child, the little girl, stays in the infants' class. She sits at a desk with her elder sister: she sits and crayons, the teacher tells me, and she seems happy enough; she is no trouble really, considering.

Laura works with me in the office. I am the administrative secretary; she is the clerical assistant. This morning I had been standing at the window watering the plants that line the sill. The ivy does badly during the summer, and I smelled sunlight burning the leaves. Outside, the infants sat on the field in a circle around their teacher, listening whilst she read them a story. Laura's toddler sat motionless; legs crossed, hands in her lap.

'How old is your little girl now?' I asked Laura.

'Gemma? She's three.'

I turned back to my typewriter. Laura, at the photocopier, lifted the cover and placed a sheet of paper beneath it before lowering it and pressing a button; then she lifted the cover again and retrieved the paper, moving it to a new pile and reaching for the next sheet. Mr James, the headmaster, says she tries hard. He told County Hall that we required extra clerical help, that he could not implement his changes without it, and because he was new they agreed. So three months ago Laura Chadwick arrived as our clerical assistant. And every day for the last three weeks she has brought that child in with her. Why?

It is quiet this afternoon. Mr James has taken his class onto the field to play rounders. One of the fielding team, Lucy, stands near my window. She is ten and due to leave at the end of term. Her limbs, shaded with freckles, are pin thin and over long. She fidgets. She turns this way and that, shifting from foot to foot, shielding her pained eyes from the sun. Her cardigan droops, trails, the sleeves knotted around her waist. She picks for a while at a scab on her elbow. Sometimes she signs or mouths messages at distant friends, or she tracks planes drifting across the sky. Occasionally, when she needs to, she watches for the ball. There is little for me to do in the office this afternoon and earlier I visited the infants' class to have a word with their teacher, Isobel.

The infants were quiet, painting pictures, hardly looking at me as I entered. They are taught in the new classroom which was added to the main building ten years ago and is reached via the cloakroom. The windows in the classroom were open and the air outside lay heavy with pollen. Sunlight burned the dust on the slats of the blinds. The room smelled still of lunch — of roast, of slabs of meat in aluminium tray, of greens — despite the hatch being closed and the tables cleared and wiped. The beakers, yellow and green and bearing teeth marks around the rim, had been returned to the tray by the sink. The infants have their own large sink. They have their own toilets too — a pink door and a blue one. The children in the other classes use the toilets outside and around the back.

'Clearing-up time,' Isobel called. 'Chop chop, don't forget to rinse the pots; brushes in the box by the sink, and pictures over there please.' She turned to me as the children scraped their chairs across the floor.

I lowered my voice as I spoke. The little Polish boy, I told her, had been taken into Great Ormond Street.

'Yes,' she said. She reached across her desk for a pen, a paper clip, a drawing pin.

'What do we know about his chances?'

The pen and paper clip and drawing pin dropped from one hand to the other and she ran her fingers through her hair.

'Not much,' she replied. 'No one knows much at all; his mother doesn't understand.'

One of the infants, Gareth Woods, interrupted us. 'Look at my picture.' He stretched a soggy painting between opened arms.

'That's lovely, Gareth,' I said, 'especially this bit here.'

The children paint houses with four windows, a door and a chimney; everything bordered by a blue strip of sky and a strip of green grass.

I turned to Isobel.

'How are things with Laura Chadwick's children?' I asked.

'Fine, no problems, they're quiet little kids, good little things.' Isobel never has a bad word for anyone or anything. She hasn't been in the job long enough. Laura's eldest child passed us as we spoke, a paint brush in her fist.

'Hello Kirsty,' I said, 'and how are you today?'

'All right,' she replied.


'That's a nice picture,' I said.

Kirsty's eyes searched among the crowds at the end of the day for her mother. Those who walk to school to collect their children gather in the playground in groups of three or four, laughing and gossiping, younger children parked beside in pushchairs. Eventually they pull away, shouting their cheerios, backing the pushchairs out of the crowds and heading for the shop and for home. They glance around as they leave, grabbing children who dart past and nudging those who are standing still, and checking that they have them all; all children to be collected on rota or for favours. Then they move away up the road, cotton dresses billowing. Other mothers arrive from town or from the Causeway in cars with dogs in the back. They have tight jeans, sunglasses and highlighted hair, and walk with a wiggle into the playground.

'That's a nice picture,' I said to Kirsty.

'It's my house,' she said.

Four windows, a door and a chimney.

People say that a mother shouldn't take a job if she can't provide arrangements for her children. I was lucky, I only ever had one child: Helen. Laura Chadwick has three — Kirsty, Gemma, and baby Steven — and three children under five is a lot for anyone to cope with. I only ever had one and that was enough for me. Laura and her mother live in the same row of council houses which stretch from the village up the hill. Laura's mother, Mrs Miller, looks after Laura's baby each day and until recently she had looked after Gemma too.

I have lived in this village since my marriage twenty-eight years ago. It is not my home; it was my husband's home; he was brought up less than five miles from here. He thought it important that children should grow up in the countryside so until recently it was Helen's home too. Now I can afford to run a car but I never had one when Helen was a child; trudging the two miles and back into town with the pram, or taking her in the evenings on buses to ballet classes. Now I drive most evenings into town to check on my mother-in-law, to pick up her washing and see what she needs.

Today was the zoo trip. I went along to help. Isobel stayed with her class and with any others who could not go: David had a hospital appointment; Alex was off early up North to see his father;

the Beetchams couldn't afford it; Jane Clement's mother disapproved. The trip was expensive and for many families there are two or more to pay for — two Fergusons, two Grays, two Lyles, three Inghams, three Careys, and the Lintons and Hegleys together. Mr James should not expect them to afford it. It is not easy to tell a child that he or she can't go on a trip with friends. They have been talking of it here for weeks; and they will write about it for weeks, too, afterwards — *my favourite animal, my picture of a zebra*, and, where the older children are concerned, *the incredible gestation period of the elephant*. He doesn't realise how hard up some of these families are; or he doesn't care. He plans to introduce a school uniform next year.

It's tidier, he says.

Helen was always tidy, I saw to that; a uniform wasn't necessary. It is not difficult to have a tidy child, and most of the parents around here are good parents.

Besides, I told him, there is nothing as untidy as an improperly worn uniform, an ill-fitting one, a skimped one.

A sense of identity, he told me. He wants a sense of identity, of loyalty, of respect.

An admission of his failure, surely?

The children seemed to have enjoyed the journey. On their return they were quiet, restful, half-slipped down over large seats and ingeniously curled at the bottom with the headrest jutting above their heads. They lay in a damp litter of coats, lulled by the engine, the hiss of rainwater around the wheels and the muted rhythms of London. Scenes flickered across the grey glass. The children turned from the smell of the dusty diamond-patterned seats and pressed their noses against the windows, placed their fingertips on the wet glass and traced the zig-zag of the bike couriers; the steps of the stringy black man, long-legged in jeans and leading a child by the hand, the steps of the white women with shopping trolleys and limbs of wriggling cellulite.

Children love the freedom found behind the high-backed seats and they crowd at the back of the coach. The back seat was claimed on this occasion by the older girls who passed a transistor radio between them. Mr James sat in the front seat chatting to the driver and consulting his wristwatch, the world at his feet. He keeps a list of those known to suffer travel sickness, and these individuals were placed with me with appropriate medication and a bucket.

It was wet. A sludgy summer rain fell on and off throughout the day, collecting in pools on the tarmac. Plans for a lunchtime picnic were shelved. We ate in the covered area set aside for school parties. I was thankful for my coffee. The children rustled paper bags, and delved; avoiding sandwiches and going for KitKats. Mr James had written to parents reminding them to provide a packed lunch. I was not hungry so I shared mine with Eleanor whose mother had forgotten. She held a salad sandwich in both hands, gnawing at it, her eyes moving occasionally, briefly, before returning to mine. She took tiny bites, anticipating the tomato. The others popped crisp bags and rolled silver foil into balls before flicking them at friends. I collected apple cores. It was my job. I know what is expected of me.

Get back into your groups, Mr James said after lunch. Find your partner. They work in pairs, he told me. There wasn't much work left for the afternoon. The children were to be allowed to do as they pleased, to go where they wanted, as long as the whole group could agree. Jamie, however, was not to go near reptiles. He has a phobia. His mother had written a note.

Mr James had asked parents to restrict pocket money: one pound seemed reasonable, he said. He was largely ignored. Anything not spent on Cornettos at lunchtime was spent in the gift shop at the end of the day. The children were eager to spend and they spent on postcards, pens and pencils: postcards of gorillas, polar bear pencil sharpeners. They crowded around each other, circling and ducking, reaching out across the counter and along the shelves, reaching for the lady at the till with coins held like pebbles between the tips of their fingers. They grasped, enfolding trinkets in one hand while seeking with the other, and in this other hand they spread their wares, poking, comparing, considering. When a decision was reached they either bagsied or replaced it.

Careful, children, we'd say. Watch what you're doing and keep out of the way please.

After purchasing they waited for friends, collecting in groups outside, opening their paper bags and peering inside and checking.

Stan drove the coach. Every Thursday he drives the children to the swimming pool. His wife works part time in the chip shop, her two black poodles waiting for her on a travel rug in the back of the car. He and his wife had two boys, one of whom emigrated whilst the other is a policeman in Walthamstow with children of his own. In the fifties Stan drove at the Elstree studios. He says he knew the stars: Diana Dors was his favourite, a great lass; but she swore like a trooper and Stan doesn't like swearing in a woman. And he once had lunch with Ronald Reagan. Ronnie told him that America was the land of opportunity. Stan's main customers these days are the schools during term time; and, at other times, the mental hospital. He takes the long-stay patients on day trips and they wet the seats.

Kids come and go, don't they, he said to me as they filed past us to their seats. Do you miss any of them? he asked. You must have seen so many, you've been in the job a long time.

I've been in the village longer, I reminded him.

You had a little girl, he said.

Helen. She lives in London, nearby, so I can go on the train to see her whenever I want.

How long is it now, he asked, that you've been in the job?

He would remember John. He would have known him from the pub. John didn't drink but he liked to go along on Friday evenings. I don't think Stan drinks either but perhaps he too likes a few hours out of the house on a Friday evening, a few quiet hours nodding across the bar at familiar faces.

Nearly ten years, I said.

Ten years, he said, incredulous. Ten years, is it?

John has been dead for ten years.


Mr James brought Kirsty Chadwick into the office this afternoon while Laura was at the Post Office. I fetched a bowl of warm water and some soap from the kitchen, closing the door behind me when I returned. Kirsty undressed and I helped her to wash.

Then she dressed in clean clothes from the cupboard — vest, T-shirt, knickers, ankle socks and baggy corduroy trousers. I put her clothes with the rest of the laundry. She returns the borrowed clothes in a carrier bag a few days later; cleaned, always, and returned without a word. I suspect that Mrs Miller, Laura's mother, is as yet unaware of the problem Laura Chadwick is hiding; yet she walks past her mother's house at the end of the day with Kirsty dressed in someone else's clothes; and she calls at the house to collect her son. Presumably Kirsty is safely at home at that time. Presumably you can fool some of the people some of the time.

'This can't go on for ever,' Mr James said as he passed me later in the cloakroom. 'Perhaps I'll have a quiet word with Mrs Miller at some stage.'

He continued on the way to his office and I continued on my way to tea. There is no staff room but at breaktime the two teachers take a chair each and sit in the main room at the hatch. This afternoon, as usual, I joined them. Mrs Whittacker, who teaches the juniors, was speaking to one of the infants. She held a cigarette; the tops of her arms aged and mottled.

'Now, Richard,' she said, distracting him from Isobel, 'you know better than to disturb Mrs Ripley during her break.'

Richard protested, hopping: someone outside had hurt their knee.

'It's all right,' Isobel acquiesced, leaving her seat, 'I'll go.'

She followed Richard, her shoes noisy on the wooden floor.

I took the cup of tea which had been left at the hatch for me. The tea is made for us by Anna, the cook, before she leaves at half past two. I pulled up a chair, and Isobel returned. Mrs Whittacker sipped tea, momentarily closing her eyes.

'I changed Kirsty again today,' I said.

Isobel stirred her tea. 'I know.'

'Things don't seem too good, do they,' Mrs Whittacker said, her eyes red rimmed, her pupils as pale as glass. She has taught for many years at the school; and she used to teach Laura. 'Laura doesn't look too good either. And the little one — Gemma — have you noticed? It's the same with her: grubby, awfully grubby.'

'Does Kirsty say much to you about it?' I asked Isobel.

'No, nothing.' Isobel held her cup in one hand, her saucer in the other.

'It's a shame,' said Mrs Whittacker. She drew on the cigarette for a moment and then exhaled with obvious relief. 'But what can we do?'

Sort out your problems, I used to say to Helen when she came in crying; fight your own fights.

And she did. She didn't come to me much. She kept herself to herself.

She took after her father.

Us Tomlinsons, he used to say, we're all the same.


Last night I watched the Weather Man. He pointed to a satellite picture. You'll be able to tell by now, he said, what this means.

It used to be either sunshine or cloud — sun rays or raindrops stuck onto a map like fuzzy felt — but now there is wind chill factor to take into

account. It had been a miserable day so I decided
to drive into town to buy something nice for tea. I
once offered a lift to Laura as she walked through
the wind and rain towards town. Kirsty was very
young then, her cheeks were red and chapped. She
sat on her mother's knee in the car and played
with the glove compartment. Laura said very little.
She said that she didn't mind walking but that it
wasn't easy with the little one. Nothing ever is, I
replied.

I was in the car last night when I heard the
programme on child abuse. There are signs, the
woman said, to look for if you suspect child abuse.
It was noted in an article in 1946, she said, that
injuries to the arms and legs of children were in
some cases associated with injuries to the head and
the stomach, chest and mouth; and it was proposed
that these injuries had been caused by punching,
by the gripping and wrenching of limbs, by impact
against hard surfaces. The author of the article had
been not a doctor but a radiographer. Paediatricians
writing in the 1960s had drawn attention to many
other forms of abuse — emotional, sexual — and
also, *failure to thrive*: neglect is a form of abuse, the
woman said.

So there are signs, some obvious, some less so.

Take Maria Colwell as an example, said the
woman: Maria Colwell became noticeably depressed in the months prior to her death.

It seems odd to me that a child should become
depressed. I lay awake last night and listened to the
wind. Usually I turn to the wall and try to sleep.
Last night I resolved to speak as soon as possible to
Mr James.

I had asked to see Mr James in private upon his return from the class trip to the village manor house. The class returned at lunchtime carrying flip-leaf sketch books. Mr James had sought permission for the visit by writing to the owners to explain how it would complement the TV series *How We Used to Live*. Architects bought the manor several years ago and converted it into their offices.

The programme, Mr James had said in his letter, concentrates twice weekly on the Victorians.

The children had chattered prior to the visit about scullery maids and governesses, about warehouses and mills, but chattered on their return about stables and attics and water wells. Mr James indicated to me that we should enter his office.

'It happens, Mrs Tomlinson, it happens,' he said when he had heard what I had to say. He laid a pile of flip-leaf sketch books on the desktop before walking around the desk to the chair and laying his jacket across it.

'I don't see what I can do about it,' he said, looking up at me and smiling, 'but I suggest that if you are worried then you have a word with Mrs Ripley. She is, after all, the child's teacher.' He rolled up his shirt sleeves and came back across the room to open the door.

'And now,' he said at the door, 'if you'll excuse me . . .'

There is a framed photograph on the wall in the cloakroom: Victorian ladies in wide-brimmed hats on the lawn in front of the manor. Helen saw many such photographs when she was a pupil here at school. The old headmaster, Mr Thomas, loves local history. He has lived in the village for more than thirty years. He retired last year with his wife and daughter to a bungalow near the church, and the schoolhouse — which is damp — is to be demolished. Mr James lives in London. Mr Thomas knows everyone in the village, and knows their tales. He knows Mrs Churchill, who is ninety-seven; and Mrs Black, who was for many years the midwife; and Mrs Darling and her six geese, Annie, Gertie, Charlotte, Emily, Sarah and Jane. He knows the families on the council estate, having taught their children and their children's children. Many families have lived locally for generations but some settled when they relocated from London after the war; and some are rural, migratory, working seasonally on the farms and living temporarily in tied cottages. Helen and her classmates had read the school records, leaning across ledgers and tracing attendances and absences, disasters and epidemics. They had sifted through photographs — stiff, dry, brown — of children sombre in horse-drawn carts, of girls in petticoats and boys in cricket teams.

Your grandparents, Mr Thomas used to tell them, your ancestors.

There has been a school in the village for hundreds of years; located at one stage on land at Grays Farm and then later in Vineyards Lane. The present building dates from 1887. From my office window there is a view over the school field towards the woods: royal hunting grounds once, then belonging to the Church, and now privately owned. It is rumoured that the estate is patrolled by men with dogs and guns. No one has permission to visit. The owner comes to church on Sundays in a car driven by his wife. She helps him from the car to a wheelchair, and covers his knees with a rug. She is a nice lady, they say; helpful, courteous, she does the church flowers on rota. Her husband has undertaken afforestation of his land for tax purposes, planting it with a bluish bristle of pine. There had once been a valley of fields, vegetal barley brown, stretching from the school to the horizon. The horizon had been full of trees flowering and fading; drying deep red in September at the start of each school year.

Mr Thomas invited Mrs Darling to visit the school on Tuesday mornings, and until recently she had continued to do so. She brought with her on these occasions her spinning, her tangly wool, the mesh of mud and straw picked in handfuls from fences around the fields; or dried grasses, leaves, seeds, butterflies and beetles.

Natural history, Mr Thomas had called it.

Sometimes when pausing and peering through the classroom window I watched children not listening; the slightest turning of their heads betrayed by the shift of light on bright crowns of hair. They tapped their feet, chewed their lips, ran their fingertips along the grooves on their desks.

You're ungrateful, I used to tell Helen. It's not boring, it's interesting.

But for the children Mrs Darling became interesting only when her husband died: her cottage, they decided, had become haunted. For a while they would go after school to the top of her gravel drive and pass by and linger and look towards her dark windows before running screaming to the safety of the main road.

I remember an Indian summer several years ago, sudden summer rain a whiplash in still air. The children hung from the climbing frame, the bars in the crooks of their knees, their hands shielding their eyes from the glare of cloud on tarmac and steel.

You'll have water on the brain, Mrs Thomas warned them, if you're not careful.

Mrs Thomas, the headmaster's wife, came to school each playtime. She changed the children's shoes — indoor to outdoor, and outdoor to indoor — and broke up their fights and swabbed their grazes. At lunchtime she cut their food into pieces. Her daughter, Sally, cleared the plates. Sally had been damaged as a child by a vaccine; and throughout her twenties she came to school each day, standing in the playground during the winter, buttons fastened, ringing the handbell at the end of playtime. In the summer she sheltered in the shade, her feet swollen in sandals. During the Indian summer several years ago the children hung from the climbing frame and watched and waited for the man they claimed to have seen running in the distance among the trees: the man they heard about, or read about, the man in the paper; the murderer, or molester; the man, in any case, who was never caught.

Something else bothers me: the radio programme said that we repeat parenting patterns. A mother raises her child as she herself was raised, the only way she knows how, and so however hard she tries she makes the same mistakes. Time and time again in the abuse of the child there is one decisive factor: a history of abuse of the mother. An abusing parent was once an abused child. If Laura was vulnerable once she will be vulnerable still and so will her children.

Laura's family, the Miller family, is well known; it is one of the older families on the estate along with the Porter family, the Clarks, and the Lintons. The Porter boy, a window cleaner, built up a successful local business of his own; his sister, Sandra, married a married man and caused a stir. The eldest Clark child was sacked last year from the local shop for pilfering. Mrs Linton was told by the Council to tidy up her garden. But things weren't easy for Mrs Linton: she took on Mr Hegley and his two children, and she has three of her own. There are two Lintons and one Hegley in Mrs Whittacker's class. Last year Mrs Linton had another baby shortly after her father had been found hanging in the barn at Grays Farm.

Laura is one of two sisters: Laura and Cassandra. Unusual names, I thought. John and I had named our daughter Helen Christobel: Helen, I suppose, because it is a good name, and John's mother's name; I don't know why we chose Christobel. Laura had always failed to cope but her sister, Cassie, was different. Cassie was dazzling. She used to trip down the lane each morning with a satchel over one shoulder: white socks, pretty ankles, perfect legs; baby blonde hair and baby blue eyes. I knew that if I glanced from my window at ten to nine each morning I would catch a glimpse of her — the bright bob of hair and, if she turned, and if she smiled, the glitter of her eyes; and, sometimes, her nails, pink and white like marshmallows.

This is Cassie, Helen said.

And Cassie smiled. Everyone always fell for Cassie.

Today, Tuesday, I went to London. It is the half term holiday before the summer: one of my last half term holidays, and Laura Chadwick's first.

What will you be doing, I had asked her.

Nothing much, she had replied.

I drove as usual to the station, parked nearby, and bought a cheap day return to Oxford Circus. The station is last on the line and has several platforms. Tracks unravel and rest side by side in trenches lined with sand. On the train people shivered with the rhythm of the carriage. Mothers and daughters sat in pairs, clearly identifiable, almost identical except in age. They shared the same nose, perhaps, or lips, or squint. They sat wordless side by side, swaying, cradling shopping bags and reading adverts. At Tufnell Park the doors opened to shouting, and twenty or thirty children entered the carriage, racing for seats, pulling friends and pushing others out of the way. The adults followed, seriously underrepresented, grappling with collapsible pushchairs. The children wore uniforms. I recalled a news item about a parade. They settled two or three to a seat, shrieking the name of each station as we passed. The adults stood in two groups: mothers, capable in skirts and cardigans and sandals, loud in their laughter and condemnation; and officials, pinned into uniforms and conspicuous to the public. The children sprawled, and shifted only when rebuked. The officials scanned the carriage, hardly daring to look. They all left at Euston, the high-pitched voices rising like a siren as the doors opened.

I had a cup of coffee mid-morning in a fast food place. In the afternoons I go to a store and order a pot of tea and a scone or a bun. In the fast food place there was an old man in old clothes on a buttock-shaped plastic seat. He sat among crowds of shoppers and couples and workmen sharing chips or choosing orders and he unwrapped an Egg Muffin, lifting it to his mouth with both hands. He took tiny frequent bites and never once raised his eyes.

I have my favourite stores: one of them is Selfridges. My grandmother worked in Selfridges when she was a girl, and then in Heals during the war. Most of the stores have been refurbished in recent years to include piazzas and piano playing and card carrying customer enquiry desks on the fifth floor. The Ladies Rooms, however, never change; still cool and quiet, the china saucers ringing with pennies. John and I took Helen every Christmas to Selfridges to see the window displays. Once we bought a bag of roast chestnuts and sat eating them in the car.

Every year I went to London to do the Christmas shopping. Helen would stay with John, waiting for me to call at the end of the day for a lift from the station and watching me, later, as I heaved bags from the station exit to the car: bags of secrets to be hidden upon my return in the wardrobe and the airing cupboard. I loved London in the last few days before Christmas, people shunted from station to station in trains; people subdued with excitement, with tired feet and glossy carrier bags. The whole world was holding its breath, waiting for snow, watching the sky, and I knew Helen at home would be watching too. I liked white Christmases, the moments before the falling of snow when the sky was muffled and low. I liked to walk around shops that were scented with pine and crackling with wrapping paper, their cool mirrors flushed with steam from wet coats. I watched shoppers propelled inwards by rotating doors as they stopped, stunned, exhaling thawing breath and shaking droplets of rain from the giant leathery wings of umbrellas. The shops were filled with foods: fruit cake heavy with alcohol, and squashed dates, and chocolates like gems in bright foil. Long shelves in the gift departments burned with bath salts. In those days the gift soaps or guest soaps — the last resort of the Christmas shopper — were unsubtle, unsophisticated, as brittle as seaside rock and coloured caustic custard yellow or yoghurt pink. The exceptions were those I could not afford, those laid like jewels in boxes and covered with muslin and fragranced with oil of lemon and lavender and rose.

Due to an earlier incident, a voice told us, the train would be delayed. Sitting opposite me in the waiting room were four girls, aged seventeen or eighteen. Common, some people would say: nice enough, but common. Their clothes were cheap but clean. The girls, too, were clean: bright pink beneath peeling tans. Fully equipped, their range of accessories was impressive and included jackets and scarves, handbags, wallets, bracelets and rings. At the end of the waiting room there was another group of girls, beautiful girls slouching in leather. In comparison the girls opposite were tidy, their haircuts recent. They were not, however, so self-assured: lively, yes, perky, but bristling, wearing stiletto heels, their eyelashes stubby with mascara. They looked at the world through different eyes and it showed.

This afternoon, when walking through the village, I met Mr Thomas, the old headmaster. He was in his garden, kneeling on a gardening mat tending a flowerbed in the shade of a hedge. All around him the sky was bright but blistered with cloud. On the horizon flecks of silver were rising and falling, tossed this way and that by the breeze: kites let loose on a race with postcards tied to their tails; or gulls perhaps. Sometimes it is difficult to tell. His hands sought plants, moving through the undergrowth. He was sifting and weeding, his face pinched in concentration. Was it true what people said about him losing his patience towards the end of his time as headmaster? Losing his legendary patience? He had made no secret of looking forward to retirement.

He did not catch sight of me until I was there beside him, but he looked up smiling: silver grey hair and sapphire blue eyes, a handsome man once; a striking man, certainly. He rose, extending a hand. I had told Helen that his being Welsh accounted for his love of music and singing, for the afternoons she had spent sitting around a piano in a classroom warm with the muddy smell of floorboard polish. In those days everyone played and everyone sang everyday: there was no choir, no selection and discrimination, no flats and bass. Often there was no piano: Mr Thomas would accompany them instead with his accordion, wheezing and sighing and jigging. He played the organ in church. His being Welsh did not explain, however, his love of Scotland. It did not explain the songs that Helen once sang — *Over the Sea to Skye,* and *Bring Back My Bonnie to Me.* Mr Thomas had come to the village from Wales more than thirty years ago, but he was planning to retire to Scotland.

You've not sold yet then, I said as we stood together in the garden. I indicated the For Sale sign over the hedge.

He smiled and shook his head. No, he said, not yet, not yet.

He was a fair man — as teacher, administrator, colleague, and friend — and he was patient. And things come to those who wait.

How was I, he asked, and how was Helen, and the job? And, talking of the job, how was Laura Chadwick?

She has a lot to cope with, I said. Three babies and a job.

Yes, he said, she does well, really, considering, doesn't she; considering she was such a funny little thing.

He smiled at me again.

Yes, he continued, she was a funny little thing. A poor little thing, he called her; and always in the wars.

I remember her in bottle green cardigans, over-large hand-knits and skimpy hand-me-downs. I remember her bony legs bare and grey with plasters.

Let your wounds breathe, I used to tell Helen.

A loner, he called her. I remember hearing her called other things — Loony Laura, Mildew Miller — and seeing her often on the other side of the playground with her back against the wall, her hands rigid at her side, her jaw dropped and mouth open, wailing. Weepy, he called her.

You get kids like that, he said: she was never one for school, for lessons, for learning, and you get kids like that; kids with headaches, earaches, tummy aches, with poor attendance records and poor diets, he said. Some kids don't stand a chance, do they, he said.

He turned away, shaking his head. He started to walk back across the lawn towards the house.

Come in for a cup of tea, he said.

I told him that I had better be getting on.

Sally is worse, he told me, and unsteady on her feet and beginning to need more help than either he or his wife could give her.

He stopped on the lawn and turned towards me. But, still, he said, smiling, it was good to see you, to have a chat, to know that you're well.

Depression, I thought as I left, I know depression when I see it: the tiredness and tirelessness of functioning and living without alternatives, of repeating things long since meaningless. There was Laura's malaise, I thought, as well as her bumps and bruises. But there is more, there is something else, there is Laura herself: no one likes her. The others at school don't like her because she doesn't play the game: she doesn't put the kettle on, first thing, and she doesn't spread the newspaper against the typewriter and read the horoscopes aloud; she doesn't mutter about tiredness and reach in her bag for an aspirin. She doesn't play the martyr. She hasn't a cause. She doesn't resent what she is supposed to resent and she isn't ultimately thankful for her lot.

In the office, earlier, on this first day of half term, Laura had brushed past my desk: brown denim knee-length skirt, colourless shins, and Scholl sandals. She had stopped by the filing cabinet. Her hair was held at the nape of her neck by a rubber band and the ponytail was pale against the nylon blouse. She had pulled open a drawer. It has not been warm today but she had rolled up her sleeves. She had reached inside the drawer and flicked through files, her hair falling at times across her eyes. She wears mascara applied every morning it seems with one hand whilst the other scrambles eggs or brushes teeth or fastens buttons; or perhaps once applied and never removed: the inevitable, indelible mark of womanhood.

Guapa, they used to say in Spain. It means beautiful. They touched Helen's head because it is lucky in Spain to touch the head of a blonde child. Guapa, they'd say, nodding and smiling.

Yes, yes, I'd say, laying my hand on her head and running her hair through my fingers.

A lovely baby, people said, such a pretty little girl.

But people always say that: they peer into the pram and tell you how lucky you are.

But Helen *was* pretty. I remember making her a cake for her sixteenth birthday. She hadn't had a birthday cake for a few years, she was too grown up, but when she was sixteen I made her a cake just like the ones we used to have with whipped cream and chocolate flakes. She wouldn't eat it.

I can't eat that, she said, I'll get fat.

No, you won't, people used to say to her, you're not the type, you've no worries, you're one of the lucky ones.

I remember our first holiday abroad, when Helen was three years old. John wanted her to have all the opportunities we never had.

Why go abroad? Mr Thomas used to ask me. He holidayed each year in Scotland and talked of lochs and burns, highlands and lowlands, folklore and folktales; and caravanning and camping and waterproofs and good strong walking boots.

Why go abroad? Why airports and beaches, why rubber rings and water wings, patatas fritas and small bread rolls on your side plate at every meal? Why bidets?

I remember bread rolls and napkin rings, starched white table cloths and a breeze breathing through net curtains. I remember the sounds from the pool on the terrace outside. I remember Helen gasping as we lowered her into the water, as it washed over her, over her navy blue swimming costume: the one with the frill, her favourite, the one she had chosen.

It's too heavy, I had told her as we packed. It'll be too hot.

But I like it, she had insisted.

Oh, go on, let her, her father added.

I remember Helen in Uvistan Number Nine, well protected, slippery; oiled and wriggly, peeled and mottled and freckled. Sunkisses, my mother called freckles: Helen sunkissed, Helen blonder than blonde on the beach, Helen in a thousand photographs pink and gold and with rows of perfect teeth and perfect fingers and toes. And I remember saving, too. It had been a bad year. We had already raided the electricity jar to buy John a new suit for a friend's wedding. So I remember saving.

But it was worth it, wasn't it, John had said.

Oh yes, it was worth it.

John took Helen everywhere with him. She went with him at weekends to motor races; and often she went with him on weekdays when he drove into London to make deliveries. Over several years they watched the renovation of St Katharine's dock. They visited museums, and towers and palaces, and queued for hours outside the Tutankhamun exhibition. They went to shows, the Boat Show and Ideal Home Exhibition and, in November, the Lord Mayor's Show, where they would find a place each year among the crowds on the pavement in the drizzle. On summer Sundays they watched gliders from the South Downs.

We spent our time together, Helen and I, when she was very young, in the park, on the roundabout and at the pond feeding ducks with crusts. I went with Helen most mornings into town to the clinic or the library or the shops. It was a pleasant walk to town in summertime or late spring or early autumn, the road winding under tall trees. On our way home we would stop at the baker's and Helen would choose cheesecakes with a tangly topping of sugar strands; or traffic light jam tarts or cornets of marshmallow and hundreds-and-thousands. She never gave me much trouble, even when she was older. She tended to go to John if she needed anything. And not long after he went, she went too.

The children paint onto sheets of paper and then cover them with waxy black crayon; then they scratch and gouge until the colours reappear: a trick learned from the peripatetic art teacher. They often choose to do it; and today, I could tell, they had chosen. I ran close to the outside of the building, twisting away from the rain, sidestepping puddles, while inside the classroom the children sat at tables cleared of books and covered with newspaper and paint pots and brushes and pallets. Their heads were bowed as they chipped and scraped. Mrs Whittacker was sitting at her desk reading women's magazines. The children are often allowed to choose what to do at the end of a long, wet day.

Can we talk? I asked Mr James when I arrived back in the office.

What about? he said. He had stopped in the doorway. He was leaving, a pile of papers under one arm.

It's important, I said.

Yes, of course, he said. He had turned to face me, his hand on the door handle, his shirt half out of his trousers and chalk on his sleeve. It was Going Home Time. Behind him in the cloakroom the children were flinging satchels, one of which landed at his feet after skidding across the tiles. He turned to face them. I'm going to get very angry, he said. He kicked at the satchel. Pick it up, he said to one of the children.

He stepped back into the office and closed the door.

So what can I do for you? he asked.

It's about Laura, I said. I told him about Laura and he leaned back against the door, nodding as I spoke. His head dropped forward little by little until it hung: this was Mr James weighed down by responsibilities, Mr James giving due consideration to a problem.

I don't doubt that you've thought very carefully about all of this, he said eventually, and you've certainly come up with some very interesting conclusions. But you and I both know, he said, that there are proper channels and correct procedures.

It was something he often said; and he went on to say all other things I've heard him say so often in the months that I have been typing his letters.

In cases such as these, he said, you should let sleeping dogs lie.

I tried to explain about Laura: it was not that she had been neglected; far from it. Mildew Miller, they had called her, but she had always seemed so clean to me; her skin scrubbed dry, her hair rubbed to a shine. She had been cleaner than Helen, no doubt. Helen had liked bubble bath and perfumes and powders and lotions: upstairs after baths she had moved barefoot around the rooms in her towelling robe, looking for the things I had forgotten I had, the gift sets and trial offers, and dabbing her wrists and neck and the crooks of her knees.

And Laura was well dressed, in a way: vest and winter woollies and, in summer, cotton dresses with geometric prints in amber and jade. Her clothes had lasted well: they came from jumble sales and Mrs Miller would have hunted hard for them. I remember her waiting in the playground each morning at the gate, watching Laura and calling her over; taking hold of her and tugging, shifting the coat on her shoulders, straightening the collar and sleeves, and muttering: *Another coat for you, Madam; stop growing so fast.*

Laura was well fed, although it never showed. She was at home at the same time each evening for a cooked meal: meat and potatoes and peas, Helen had told me, and a pudding too — sponge and custard. Helen had sometimes had tea with Cassie. Cassie would have asked her mother for egg and soldiers, for welsh rarebit or salad or sandwiches and a pot of yoghurt; and she would have been given them. Laura would have sat in front of the meat and potatoes and peas until her plate was taken away.

I can't eat it all, she used to say.

Well, if you can't eat it all, Mrs Miller would reply, then you can't eat any pudding, can you? You can go without.

She was well brought up: no earrings, no make-up, no back-chat. She was well cared for, considering; considering her father was away from time to time, for weeks at a time, for months perhaps, sometimes working and sometimes not. He works — when he works — in the construction industry, someone once told me. Often he returned at the end of the week, late, tired. At other times he was at home for weeks or months.

Mrs Miller cleaned at the houses on the Causeway. During school holidays Laura had accompanied her, playing in the gardens in the summer and in the winter moving quietly from room to room behind her. Mrs Miller took Laura everywhere with her; she never left her alone with anyone. Wherever Laura was, Mrs Miller came promptly to fetch her. She arrived early at Helen's birthday parties, at half past five instead of six o'clock, and stood wedged in the doorway while Laura begged her to wait for the cake to be cut and parcelled in paper napkins, and for the take-home gifts and balloons to be distributed. Cassie, being older, was allowed to stay.

It is difficult to explain about Laura. What was odd was not that she cried so often but that she cried so often alone and not in the playground like the others. She didn't cry like the others when they lost at games or tripped and fell; not like the other children noisy with frustration and wounded pride but easily consoled.

Always snivelling in corners, her teachers said of her.

Look at you, her mother used to say, you're a mess, you're no good to anyone looking like that. Smarten yourself up a bit, make an effort, because the world doesn't owe you a living.

Laura went to work in the shoe shop on the High Street when she left school, and she met Billy Chadwick. Billy was the first boy to take her to pictures on Friday nights and to visit her at home on Sunday afternoons. They married at eighteen and he moved into her room in her parent's house.

I'll not have her getting pregnant under my roof, her mother had said. She said it in Tesco's as we queued at the cooked meats counter.

Pandemonium, she said, standing with her hands on her hips; her 'shopper' — waterproof tartan with wheels — at her side.

There isn't enough room for us all as it is, she finished.

But Laura was pregnant straight away and straight into smocks, picking her way along the trestle tables at the village hall craft fairs, picking out crocheted bunnies and fluffy pom-poms for hanging in cots and prams. The Council agreed to house the couple but under the usual conditions: the baby has to be born alive before the parents can jump the queue.

That's all very well, Mr James said to me, but it's all in the past, it doesn't matter now.

It matters, I said. If Laura was vulnerable once, she is vulnerable still, and so are her children; she needs to talk.

There is a lot of talk around at the moment, he replied, and women such as yourself, Mrs Tomlinson, women with time on their hands and a wide knowledge of community affairs may be tempted to misinterpret things.

I told him about Laura's file, about the absences and queries, the bumps and bites and bruises: I told him my evidence.

He stepped into the middle of the room.

This is intolerable, he said, quite intolerable. It was wrong, he said, you were wrong, Mrs Tomlinson, you did wrong. You had no right, Mrs Tomlinson, you should never have read that file. Confidential material, he said, and you know it.

He turned his back to me and opened the door.

I thought you could be trusted, he said, but obviously not; and I need staff whom I can trust, Mrs Tomlinson.

He passed through the doorway and turned again to face me, his hand on the door handle.

I can't imagine, he said, shaking his head, how you gained access to it. Gained access? I said. *Gained access?* I put the out-of-date files in the old schoolhouse, I said, upstairs in the back bedroom, in the chest of drawers to the right of the fireplace; if you ever want to read them, I said, if you should ever find you need to.

Laura is inadequate, he said as he left. It surprises me that you haven't thought of self-inflicted injury because her case has all the hallmarks of it.

Cassie dazzled Helen.

They were five years old, twenty years ago, in the garden. It was very hot and very bright; mid-afternoon in July or August or early September, during school holidays. Helen stood at Cassie's side.

'This is Cassie,' she said, smiling.

Cassie blazed, her hair sweeping in the sunlight as she turned. She turned and glanced at me, shielding her eyes.

'Hello Mrs Tomlinson,' she said.

And I remember that on so many other occasions, and so often through the years, Cassie was pale and pink, soft and smooth; that she shimmered. But I know that when I first saw her, when I had first glimpsed her in the garden, she had blazed.

Helen had birthday parties. I made birthday cakes, Victoria sponges with raspberry jam and chunks of blue and white icing like those brought home in handfuls of paper napkin from other children's parties. In later years I bought cakes decorated as hedgehogs or Hector-the-dogs from the bakery in the High Street. And later still, for her grown-up birthday teas with myself and John and perhaps with a friend or two of hers, a boyfriend perhaps, she would have a chocolate flake cake. Cassie came to Helen's sixth birthday party in scarlet hotpants. She played in the garden with the other little girls. The mothers who had come to help were in the living room smoothing paper tablecloths across tables and pouring beakerfuls of cherryade, leaning against the window sills and nibbling at sausage rolls and twiglets. The children had taken outside with them fistfuls of iced gems. The sandwiches were left, of course — the rolls and baps of egg and cress, cheese and tomato, fishpaste or ham — and I would have had them later for supper. I stood at the kitchen window that day and rinsed down the sink the dregs of raspberry ripple icecream from the bowls. I watched Cassie riding Helen's new bike around and around the lawn. Now I feel sure that if Laura had ever wanted to harm herself then the explanation must lie with Cassie.

The school field has been mown; the dried clippings rolled hot and sweet by the breeze. I sit by the window, typing, fingers running over keys, the form and rhythm of words and phrases familiar. The window is open. I can hear children elsewhere in the building chanting in unison their end of afternoon prayers; standing, no doubt, beside tables cleared of everything except upturned chairs. Everything is cleared into lockers, little wooden drawers bearing names — Harriet, Julie, Paul, Ryan — and stickers, sometimes of a smiling sun, or a black cat wearing a ribbon, or a postman perhaps or a rosy red apple.

Take special care of felt tips, Mrs Whittacker says when the children clear the table. Replace the caps tightly.

Laura is across the room from me, filing. She takes each document from the tray and lays it on a nearby table. And then she approaches it for clues, her forefinger feeling along each line, her eyes flicking from word to word; reciting, soundlessly, with a rush of breath. When she has found her clue and made the decision where to file it she closes her mouth, withdraws her finger and straightens, lifting the document and turning and moving towards the filing cabinet. But with one of the documents she is unable to make a decision. She slows, silent, her finger back and forth across the page.

'Try "Fund Raising",' I say.

She glances at me, straightens, lifts the document and turns.

'How's Cassie?' I ask her.

Laura stops, still, the piece of paper fluttering for an instant at the end of her extended arm. She does not turn to face me.

'All right,' she replies.

And then she raises her arm, drops the paper back into the tray and turns towards the door. She is about to leave.

'As thick as thieves,' I say.

She is lifting her jacket from the hook on the door.

'Who?' She speaks quietly.

'Cassie and Helen, of course,' I say, my fingers staccato on the keyboard. 'You do remember, don't you?' I say. 'Don't you remember? Helen and Cassie?'

I remember Helen and Cassie at school, and at Brownies: in school uniform, with cowslip in their hair, and in the school play with pipe-cleaner haloes and wings of tin-foil; at Brownies as elves or sprites or buttercups or whatever they were. And at Guide camp later, caught with cigarettes behind the Portaloo; and at secondary school, with identical, non-regulation raincoats.

'Do you remember?' I say. I tell Laura that I used to regard Cassie as a bad influence. 'I admit it,' I say, and I laugh.

Laura has stopped, standing pressed up against the door, hands behind her back gripping the handle, her jacket trailing by her feet. Her head hangs. She regards me from under hair which falls across her eyes, jabbing at it with her fingers. I tell her that I am to visit Helen at the weekend. Eventually she asks me. 'How is Helen?'

'Oh,' I say, smiling, peeling the sheet of paper from the typewriter, releasing it with a snap, 'you know Helen . . .'


Pop in, Helen says, if you're passing.

I visited her in the spring when she had just moved into her flat. I spent the afternoon looking for it, arriving at Paddington Station at lunchtime and walking westwards. I passed supermarkets with names I did not recognise, supermarkets open late, with bread — french loaves, packets of pitta — at the tills alongside cigarettes, confectionery, alcohol. I was hungry. Eventually I entered one of them and walked along aisles lined with fridges containing cans of drink and pots of yoghurt, all flavours, and cottage cheese, all varieties, and humous, tzatziki, taramasalata. The freezers along the back wall were filled with plastic tubs of icecream in yellow, pink and brown. I decided on a bar of chocolate. At the till most people were without trolleys. They shopped singly: pensioners with sardines and Mr Kipling cakes — Farmhouse Country or Jam Sandwich — and young people with bread and biscuits and an apple, perhaps, or a coke.

Further west the streets and crescents were lined with town houses, four-storey houses in rows sweeping towards Holland Park; rows painted white and pink in places, or blue, or lemon. Town houses with ample parking spaces and paving and railings; each ground floor secluded, steps and porches shaded by palms, walls hot with clematis; each house with full-length windows, glass panelling at the front and in the distance at the back; and, in between, the glimmer of a room dim with mahogany. And in between the rows of houses, at the back, were valleys of garden: private garden, landscaped and for residents only, for key holders busy at six with pre-dinner drinks.

In Bayswater, houses had become flats, hotels or hostels; crumbling, the guttering splintering and sagging, the paint flaking from columns. The windows were open, curtains or blinds secured against the jangle of the West London afternoon. The residents, mothers and children, sat on the front steps with their toes in the moss between the stones, pushchairs parked at their sides; close to the bins stacked by the walls, in patches of sunlight and shadow.

Helen had returned home from work shortly before I arrived. There were underclothes, recently rinsed, hanging in the bathroom to dry. She had washed her hair and secured it, still damp, with a large red plastic clip. She has fine hair, flyaway. The ends, I noticed, were lighter than the roots but whether due to dye or to sunlight I did not know. She dyes it at times; she has dyed it before. She had also changed her clothes before I arrived, changed out of her work clothes and into a pair of over-large dungarees and a yellow striped T-shirt.

She had been preparing a sandwich for her tea, the six-thirty local television news programme chatty and light-hearted in the background. The windows were open; the curtains shifting noiselessly, sagging with dust rising from the street below and upsetting a pot plant. I had rung the doorbell and she had opened her first floor window a little wider, lifting it with difficulty. She had seen me and then disappeared; and after a moment I had heard her clatter down the stairs and release the chain.

She offered to make me a sandwich.

'Can I help?' I asked.

'I don't think so.'

She continued, slipping back and forth across the room, fetching and twisting and turning; the fridge door closing several times with a thud. She squeezed ice cubes from a plastic tray into two beakers: orange juice for me, and lemon PLJ for herself.

'PLJ?'

Although she denies it she has a sweet tooth. She takes after her father. It is his mother who drinks PLJ and only when she is poorly.

'It's refreshing,' she said. 'I have a taste in my mouth.' She pulled a face.

'What kind of taste?'

'Just a taste.'

She continued, shuffling in loose espadrilles, her feet bare; a bangle spinning around her wrist. She had recently separated from her boyfriend, Alex. He had left her and she had said very little about it. Her eyes, usually colourful, were dense. She was un-aware, I suspect, that her misery was so apparent. It was apparent from, among other things, the state of her nails. She was unaware that her misery had marked her, that she was no longer the girl he had left, loving and loveable. I suspect she wanted him to find her as he had left her, should he ever return.

Cassie wasn't a bad kid, Laura had said.

She had said it as I stood at the window, watering the plants. Outside the grass had reflected sunlight, and heat had risen over distant trees.

Inside, in Mr James's classroom, the children had been singing to the chimes of the piano: *The Lord God made them all.* Laura had stood in shadow, her eyes large and pale like eggshells.

Cassie wasn't a bad kid, she said, really.

We were sitting after lunch in the playground, Isobel, Mrs Whittacker and I, facing the sun, our chairs against the wall. At our feet were cups and saucers, empty, smeared with milk along the rim or down the sides. In the kitchen behind us water streamed into steel sinks. We had had salad for lunch, with crisps, and then iced buns: treats for the children. The children were playing in the playground and on the field. Marcia Linton and Paula Hegley were clapping and singing, facing each other: hands together, clapping, and then reaching for each other, slapping; reaching to the right and then to the left, to the right and the left, and meeting in the middle, pushing against each other's palms:

> My aunty told her
> I kissed a soldier.

Mrs Whittacker offered her wrist to me and then to Isobel: perfume, duty-free, brought back by her son from his holiday.

'A lovely place,' she said. 'You should see the photos. Self catering: they prefer it and I can't say I blame them because the last time I was abroad the dining room was spotless but the portions were small. And it will be their last good holiday for a while because Lesley's planning a baby. A baby at nineteen; it's far too young; you should be off enjoying yourself at nineteen.'

She paused.

'Mind you,' she added, 'some people say it's the best time, of course, to get them over with.'

We sat in silence for a moment.

'So, anyway,' she said, 'no more size ten jeans for Lesley: she plans to leave work at Christmas. She has never liked the job.'

'And what about Tim?' asked Isobel. 'What's your Tim doing for a holiday this year?'

Mrs Whittacker laughed. 'Oh, my youngest likes a different sort of holiday,' she replied. 'He's not one for lying around on beaches. He was planning on canoeing in France, with Mike, his best friend, but Mike is getting married. So go with Jeff, I said. Jeff's another friend. Jeff'll go with you, I said. But Jeff's planning a holiday with Carol, he said. So twist his arm, I said. You take Mandy, I said, and he takes Carol: simple.'

At the far end of the playground the girls were skipping. Clare and Eleanor turned the long rope between them, winding it through the air and striking the concrete with a regular rhythm. The others watched the rise and fall, waiting in line, recounting the rhyme — o-u-t spells OUT — before the next in line enters the arc, closing her eyes, hoping and praying that she won't miss, misjudge, trip or tangle.

The office window was open behind us. I stood up and walked over to it. Laura was inside at the desk, a round of sandwiches in clingfilm on a saucer in front of her. She looked up at the window as I approached. 'Come outside,' I said. 'Bring a chair.'

I returned to my seat. Mrs Whittacker was lighting a cigarette. She breathed smoke and scanned the playground. Her eyes were almost clear in the sunlight, her irises flaws beneath the surface.

'Kirsty,' she called out, 'Kirsty Chadwick.'

Kirsty stopped, turning away from her friends Alice and Clare, and dropping a tennis ball from her hands. Alice stooped behind her and retrieved it.

'Kirsty, do your laces up please, properly.' Mrs Whittacker jabbed with her cigarette in the direction of Kirsty's shoes. 'There's a good girl.'

Everyone had imagined that Cassie would be the first of her classmates to get married; or, at least, the first to get pregnant.

She knows it all, her teachers used to say of her.

She was surrounded by friends and classmates whenever she sat on the school field plucking petals from a flower — he loves me, he loves me not — or whenever she watched the older children playing tennis; and whenever she doodled in her notebook, hearts and flowers, or fastened her hair, or hummed or sang. She had her favourite friends: big silent Caroline, and tiny Tamara. Caroline and Tamara would stand beside her on the field when she watched the boys playing football. She left the village many years ago but has only recently married. She is now in Reading, in a semi, her husband in the Forces.

'I thought Cassie would be the first to get married,' I said to Mrs Whittacker as we sat together in the sun waiting for Laura to join us.

Mrs Whittacker shrugged. 'Which only goes to show,' she replied.

I remember how Cassie knew all the gossip; and she knew all the best jokes. She was clever at school, too: quick, methodical, her answers correct and completed ahead of time. She was not Helen's best friend, however. Helen's best friend was Jackie Smith. Jackie's mother was Italian, from Naples; a nurse at the local hospital. Jackie's father had once worked at the hospital as a porter. Jackie spoke no Italian, but to Helen she was exotically foreign because of the silver bracelet that she had worn on her wrist since her christening. But Jackie was like any other little girl in the village, prancing in patent leather party shoes and painting her nails with her mother's leftover polish or the clear polish from kiddies' kits, from the cellophane wrapped sets of handmirrors and combs. She drew on her hands, too, with green felt tip pen, as all the little girls did. Cassie, when she was older, I remember, would etch the initials of her boyfriends with the sharp end of a pair of compasses into her arm.

'Fancy seeing you here,' I said.

Laura had walked with Kirsty and Gemma from the school to the shop. They had stepped ahead of me through the shadows in the lane.

At the shop Laura had bought cat food: two tins of chicken liver.

'Cats,' said Mrs Donovan, totalling the bill, 'they end up costing you more than the rest of the family put together.'

'And bread,' Laura said suddenly, 'I forgot the bread. A loaf of bread, please.'

Kirsty was asking for chocolate.

'I've only white bread left,' said Mrs Donovan, placing a loaf on the counter. She totalled the bill once again and Laura paid.

'I was after bread as well,' I said when it came to my turn.

'I've only the white.'

'That'll do,' I said.

Outside the shop Laura strapped Gemma into the pushchair and placed the two tins in her lap. She handed Kirsty the loaf. Kirsty dropped it. Laura picked it up and balanced it on top of the tins.

'Here,' I said, stepping from the shop and closing the door behind me, 'let me take it.'

'No,' she said, 'it's all right, we can manage.'

'No,' I said, approaching her, 'let me take it, just to the end of the road.'

Earlier this afternoon I offered to take home Laura's girls because she had become unwell.

'What's the matter?' I asked her. She had stopped in the middle of the office and reached for the desk. She leaned heavily, folding herself over it.

'Nothing,' she replied, without looking at me.

'Feeling faint?'

'A bit.'

Momentarily she weakened, falling a little before pushing hard against the desktop and straightening herself, breathing, and reeling. Her shoulders dropped when she exhaled. And then she moved slowly to her chair. I fetched some water.

'You had better stay as you are,' I told her as I handed her the glass. 'You had better stay sitting for a while.'

'No,' she replied, after swallowing. 'I can't, I have to fetch Steven from my mother's straight after school.'

'It can wait.'

'No it can't, not today, she has a hospital appointment in town at four o'clock.'

It was almost half past three. Laura rose, wincing, her forehead thickening and puckering like rind.

'Sit down,' I said.

She stooped, her breathing irregular.

'Sit down,' I repeated, 'and I'll go to your mother's to fetch Steven. I'll take the girls with me. We'll wait at your house and you can follow when you're able.'

'So, did you have a nice day?'

The pushchair rattled, and Kirsty's feet in sandals pattered over small stones and grit and glass.

'I saw you out on the field,' I continued, 'after lunch, with Mrs Ripley, making daisy chains. I used to make daisy chains when I was a girl.'

'Which house is grandma's?' I asked her before I remembered.

We had turned into Park Road, lined on both sides with houses built during the nineteen-fifties: semi-detached, pebble-dashed, each with a front gate and garden and path to the front door. Each door was within a porch and reached in most cases by way of a doormat bearing the word *welcome*. Most doors were painted red or blue, but some had been replaced by owner-occupiers favouring mock-Georgian panelling with gilt knockers. The porches were littered with children's wellies; and on each wall was a wooden meter cabinet — handy, no doubt, for milk bottles and spare keys. The window of each upstairs landing displayed a vase, and the bathroom window at the side of each house contained frosted glass, a blind, and an extractor fan.

Mrs Miller, opening her front door, stopped. She stared. Her jaw sagged. 'Well it's just as well that you were around,' she said when I had explained. 'You'd better come in.'

She moved aside, stepping back into the hallway. One hand remained on the door, and the other gestured over the threshold. The hand on the door was heavy with rings on the third finger and with charms on a chain around the wrist.

'Perhaps not,' I replied. I explained that Laura would not be long.

'So if you'll just hand me Steven,' I said, 'I'll get going.'


Laura's front door stuck. I pushed and pulled for a moment, rattling and grating the key in the lock. Suddenly it opened, spinning back on its hinges, the letterbox jangling. The girls leapt over the doorstep, running down the hall and through a doorway at the end. Two cats appeared, sliding around a doorframe on the left and stepping from blue and white tiles onto carpet. I parked the pushchair outside the front door, applying the brake with my foot and lifting the baby clear of straps and buckles.

In the kitchen, cupboards lined the walls, those above eye-level fitted with panels of frosted glass. All woodwork was painted blue. The sink was enamel. On the draining board were cups — seven or eight, upturned. At the side of the sink was a water heater with a pair of rubber gloves over the pipe.

In the living room the girls were watching television. Gemma sat on the floor in front of an armchair. Kirsty curled on the settee, sucking her thumb.

'I'll huff and I'll puff and I'll blow your house down. . .' *Jackanory*.

'I bet you like this, don't you,' I said. 'My little girl did, and we used to watch it every day when she came home from school.'

I sat at the other end of the settee for a moment with Steven on my knee before lifting him and placing him beside his sister, and leaving for the kitchen.

I dried the cups, wiping them with a teatowel I had found on a hook by the sink and placing them on a shelf in a cupboard behind me. Through the window I watched two yellow dogs sniffing around the gatepost, and Paul Hegley wiping the windscreen of a car with a cloth. I returned to the living room. Steven having lay slumped against a cushion. He turned his head towards me as I entered. He raised himself, breathless, bubbling, and agog. I crossed the room and sat beside him.

'What a good baby,' I said.

I tickled him under his chin. He struggled to smile.

'What a lovely baby,' I said.

Kirsty looked away and gazed again at the television.

'Mummy will be home soon,' I said.

There was a clock on the mantelpiece. The time was twenty-five to five. I rose and walked towards the door.

'What does mummy like for her tea?' I asked Kirsty.

'Eggy soldiers,' she replied.


I should have known, I should have guessed; but, of course, she had told me that there was nothing wrong.

'No, nothing's wrong,' she had said, standing in front of the mirror when she had returned. 'Everything's fine, thanks.'

She turned from one side to the other, her gaze not leaving the glass, her feet not shifting on the rug; she rocked, fixing her hair, the hairgrips held between her teeth. She looked at my reflection in the mirror and smiled.

I did not know until it was announced by Mr James at the Whitsun service.

An announcement, he said, I have a special announcement to make.

His mouth widened and stretched. I was sitting with the staff on a row of wooden chairs at one side of the lectern, facing the pews. Mr James had been pacing the aisle, reading and preaching and conducting, but now he moved to the end of the row. He stood beside Laura and patted her arm.

A happy event, he said. Mrs Chadwick is expecting again.

His audience murmured appreciatively. Laura bowed her head, biting her lip and smiling.

Mrs Whittacker placed her mouth close to my ear. All hell let loose, she confided, because her mother will kill her.

And we'll be very sorry to lose you, Mr James continued.

Laura raised her head, her mouth opened, her eyes following him as he turned from her into the aisle. She swayed in his wake, one arm slightly raised. He turned, smiling and frowning, and gripped the arm; squeezing it and then releasing it.

Congratulations, he said, once again.

'Go outside,' I said to Laura, 'and I'll bring the tea on a tray.'

She sat on a chair in the shelter of the school building; the playground empty, the children in lessons. She faced the sun, her eyes closed. It had rained; sunlight lapped at puddles on the tarmac and raindrops licked the length of the bars of the climbing frame. She did not hear me approach. She sat with her legs outstretched, crossed at the ankle; four months pregnant, nearly five, and the pregnancy is inconspicuous. But still I should have guessed. When I reached her she looked up at me and smiled. I set the tray down at her feet. There were two cups and saucers on the tray, and four chocolate digestive biscuits from the staff tin. When I looked up at her she was smiling still, sunlight pale in the lace of her hair.

Laura's baby is due in the autumn. Helen was born in the autumn, and it is her favourite time of year. There is an apple tree in the garden and in the autumn the apples lie slushy, darkening with sores; or they pelt the ground, gem green and chutney tough. Helen collected them, crouching on the wet grass in her wellingtons with the washing up bowl at her side. She turned each apple in her hand, sorting the good from the bad. She didn't like stewed apple or baked apple or apple crumble but she liked Eve pudding with the sponge half cooked and sticking to her spoon.

The weather at Helen's birthday party each year was variable. Sometimes it was hot at the end of a summer of long days and late suppers, of gardens littered with paddling pools and cushions and towels discarded dewy at dusk. Sometimes it was warm, a glimmer at the end of a summer of rain at fêtes and of cancelled picnics and macintoshes. Sometimes it was cold, wet, and the children stayed indoors and played dead lions on the living room floor.

Sometimes at the end of late autumn days, or wintry days, or Sundays, we would go together for a walk, Helen and I: we would have spent the day indoors, Helen on the living room floor in droopy woollen tights, her cheeks blurred with heat and her breathing sleepy-shallow. She would pack away her toys when asked and fetch her coat. We walked, usually, through the village to the woodlands; the streets quiet, the gardens a ramshackle of late roses. The woods were filled with bonfire smoke, the ground warm beneath the crunch of leaves. Helen would run ahead, bright with cold. When we returned I would draw the curtains and prepare an early tea: on Sundays we had soup and salad. Salad in those days, the days before radicchio, consisted of cucumber, lettuce and tomato in slices on a plate; and bread and butter. Helen would watch BBC adaptations of Dickens or the Brontes and then have her bath and go to bed. I would fetch clean clothes for her from the airing cupboard and iron them ready for the morning.

The things Mrs Whittacker had whispered to me in church were true: she had told me more. We had walked together at the end of that afternoon from the gate to the main school building. She had been waiting for the last of the children to leave, watching them chided and hurried by mothers in the lane. She had been leaning on the fence, tapping her front teeth with the end of a biro. I had been across the road to post the letters. There were no longer any cars parked outside except her own — a red hatchback — and Mr James's. Isobel travels as far as the railway station with her. She had straightened when I reached the gate, turning from the road and dropping the biro into her cardigan pocket. We had walked across the playground, her weight slung between her hips with each step, her low heels — Marks and Spencer, navy blue — rapping the concrete. She had pushed her sleeves up her arms. Her hands are large and white, soft with washing up water. She covers them night and day with lotion; treating them to Oil of Ulay, she says, on high days and holidays, and with Germolene during winter.

She had told me as we walked across the playground that Mrs Miller — collecting Kirsty from school not long after Steven's birth — had talked with Isobel.

She shouldn't have any more kids, she had said of Laura.

She had said it in the cloakroom, standing in her overcoat and boots amid children eddying and excitable with models made of cardboard and sellotape and glue.

Kirsty had been standing beside her; her face up-turned one moment and down-turned the next, and something in her hands — a book or a puzzle or something.

She already has three, Mrs Miller had continued, so what would she want with another?

'An autumn baby,' I said to Laura as we drank the tea, 'a good choice.'

Helen had been born in the autumn, I told her. And John, too, and John's mother, and my mother and her brother. 'But I was born in the winter,' I said, and I laughed.

'And your brothers and sisters?' Her face gleamed, copper in places with fine hairs across the brow and along each eyelid.

'I have none,' I told her.

She was silent; her eyes were closed.

'What will you do,' I asked her, 'when the time comes? How will you manage?'

Acres of woodland reflected in her eyes as she turned to me. She smiled. 'I'll manage,' she replied. 'I expect Cassie will help.'

'Cassie? You never seemed to have been close,' I said.

She shrugged. 'We're sisters.'

Mrs Whittacker was in the kitchen when I returned the tray so I told her Laura's plans.

'Odd,' I said, 'don't you think, because they never seemed to have been close.'

She prised the lid from the biscuit tin.

'Better the devil you know,' she said.


'It must have been hell,' I said, 'to have a sister like Cassie.'

Laura smiled. 'Why do you say that?' she asked.

It was Sports Day and we were sitting on the grass. Games and races were taking place throughout the afternoon at the other end of the field. Every year the children from three other local schools would attend with their parents as spectators or volunteers. Competitors gathered in the distance. Mr James strode amongst them, shouting: 'My lot, follow me, into position, on the double.' He turned to a group of girls. 'You're not listening, are you?' he bellowed at them. '*Are* you?' One of them, Mandy Lewis, crossed the field towards him. I couldn't hear what she said to him, but I heard his reply.

'Not fair? Not fair? Of course it's fair, I don't see what you're complaining about.'

He stalked away from her into the crowd.

'Move yourself, Mandy,' he continued, his voice raised, 'and let's have a little less of a song and dance about it, thank you.'

I looked at my watch. Orange squash had to be served at half past two.

'Orange, Mrs Tomlinson,' Mr James had reminded me, 'at two-thirty please, thank you very much.'

Before coming onto the field I had filled an aluminium jug with squash, and Laura had fetched the biscuits, Nice and Garibaldi.

In weather such as this Cassie used to lie on her back in the grass, her buttons undone, her sleeves rolled up and her midriff bare, her skirt above her knees; flat, stretched, silent, her friends settling beside her.

Cassie was rarely outstanding at Sports Day but could be relied upon to perform adequately. Laura could not. On these occasions as on all others their avoidance of each other was like that of conspirators.

Now that I have a car I swim several times each week. I drive not to town — to the Sports Complex — but to an outer district of north east London where I swim in an Edwardian baths attended by very few locals. Presumably there are school parties, but not early in the morning or in the evening, and I swim during the quiet hours: serious swimmers, we are called; solitary swimmers stealing across the tiles towards the water at the very beginning or the very end of each day. The older women tend to swim in twos and threes, chatting, necks craned and heads held high. The younger women, figure conscious, raise their heads only for air but remain otherwise length after length tucked beneath the surface. There are few children during the quiet hours, but occasionally there are men diving, racing, and achieving personal bests or kicking as if at bathtime. I slip down into the water and float above china blue tiles. Somewhere in the roof there is music: *River deep mountain high, Reach out and I'll be there.* Echoes of Motown on marble. I listen, stroking the surface, pointing my toes, moving sharply across the water at first; and then, gradually, slower.

Helen enjoyed swimming. Her favourite, she claimed, and not ballet classes on Saturdays, or horse riding on Wednesdays; nor, later, tennis club or school netball.

A solitary child, John called her. Let her alone, he'd tell me, let her be.

And she sat alone, often, her head bowed over a book or a toy, a trinket, a fragment, a pine cone; and on journeys she sat apart in window seats.

Give her time, John would tell me, and she'll come around in the end.

She learned to swim during our second holiday abroad.

Waterbaby, John called her.

I reminded them each day of the hotel mealtimes but inevitably I would sit alone in the dining room, choosing the starter, the watery minestrone or fruit juice. Whenever John had joined me he would stand across the room at the french windows looking over the terrace towards the pool.

Look at her, I'd hear him say. Look at her, the waterbaby.


Cassie had not been lovable or likeable either. Dazzling, maybe, but during all those years of schooldays

and holidays and evenings spent at Brownies and
Guides, of youth club and tennis, of table tennis
and Keep Fit and Flower Arranging, of parties and
bonfires and carol singing, she never said more than
a few words to me.

Confident, people said of her. Very grown-up, very
sure of herself, and too clever by half.

'Does she know?' I had asked Laura when we sat
together at Sports Day. 'Does Cassie know yet about
the baby?'

'She should do,' she had told me, 'because I've written to her.'

Laura does not have a phone. This afternoon I spoke
to her about it as she prepared to leave with Kirsty and
Gemma. Mrs Whittacker was shouting next door at her
pupils: 'Let's get cleaned up in here, let's make sure we
get away on time, let's keep the noise down.'

'You can use my phone,' I said to Laura, 'whenever
you need to.'

'That's very kind of you, Mrs Tomlinson,' she replied. She was reaching for Gemma's hand. 'Give me
your hand,' she said to her. She bent forwards, her bag
swinging from her shoulder, her hair falling across her
eyes. Gemma ducked to dodge the bag; she clutched at
Laura; they missed each other.

'Just give me your hand.'

Gemma tottered and cowered. Laura snatched at
her. It has been a long time since anyone has held
my hand. Laura gripped Gemma's hand; Kirsty stood
apart from them both, her feet braced, hips forward
and skirt uneven across her thighs, her fingers in her
mouth.

'You'll have heard the news.' Mrs Miller spoke to me from the post office counter across the shop. Beyond her Mr Donovan worked in shadow behind glass. I had dropped in at the shop to buy bonbons.

'Bonbons?' Mrs Donovan had asked me, turning to face the shelves which lined the wall behind the counter. She had raised herself onto her toes, and felt with her hand among the jars of sweets. 'Lemon bonbons?' The hand had paused on a jar of lemon bonbons.

'No,' I said, 'not lemon. Just the plain white ones.' I scrutinised the shelves.

'You'll have heard the news about Laura,' Mrs Miller repeated. Several large denomination notes had been pushed towards her from under the glass screen. She lifted them from the counter and folded them into her purse, nodding at Mr Donovan as she turned away. She crossed the shop towards me, a bag swinging on her arm.

'You mean about the baby?' I asked her.

She stood beside me and we watched Mrs Donovan tipping bonbons from a jar onto the scales.

'No more kids,' Mrs Miller said, 'that's what Laura told me. But, of course, I didn't believe her because as far as she's concerned I'm never sure what to believe.'

Mrs Donovan lifted the pan from the scales and the bonbons trickled into a small paper bag.

'Laura is so very unreliable,' she said, 'as I'm sure you've gathered.'

Mrs Donovan handed me the bag. I thanked her, and paid.

I remarked to Mrs Miller as we walked to the door that she seemed worried.

'Yes,' she said. 'I am. Laura worries me.'

We stepped into the street.

'True, Cassie could be a proper little Madam,' she said, lifting her bag higher onto her arm, 'but she certainly knew how to take care of herself. And that's what people loved her for, and of course they did. I may well have had my hands full with Cassie but it was only the usual teenage troubles. But with Laura things were different.' We had stopped at the kerbside. 'But, then,' she said, 'you don't need me to tell you that.' We waited for cars to pass.

'Are you coming my way?' I asked her as we stepped from the kerb into the road.

'No,' she said. She smiled and patted her bag. 'Shopping, weekly shopping: the shops are open in town until eight tonight.'

'Of course,' I said, 'late night shopping.'

'And there's a bus at six,' she said, indicating the bus stop.

We reached the pavement and stood for a moment facing one another.

'Well,' I told her, 'I suppose I had better be on my way.' I stepped backwards. 'So, enjoy the shopping.'

She glanced back at the bus stop before stepping towards me. 'Sometimes,' she said, 'I'd like to wash my hands of Laura, I really would, once and for all.' The bag had slipped down her arm. 'I've spent my life looking out for her,' she said. 'But, then, it wouldn't be Laura who would suffer, would it: it would be Billy, poor Billy, I don't blame Billy. And it would be those poor kids of hers. And those kids suffer enough: she doesn't even keep them clean, you know, and there's no excuse for that sort of thing, is there, Mrs Tomlinson.' She raised the bag, and turned towards the bus stop. 'It's not difficult, is it, Mrs Tomlinson,' she said as she left me, 'to keep a child clean.'

Laura left after lunch for a clinic appointment in town. She left after having scraped the last of the leftover rhubarb and custard from the bowls into the bucket: the children refer to the bucket as *the pigbin*; Mr James calls it *waste disposal*. She intended that her mother should collect Kirsty and Gemma from school at the end of the afternoon.

'You can leave them with me,' I said, 'and I'll see as I did before that they get home.'

Many of the children who live nearer go to the park after school. In the autumn, at the start of each school year, they bring plastic containers — icecream cartons and tupperware — in which to collect blackberries.

'Your mum can makes pies with them,' they tell each other, initiating a craze at the start of each year. 'Blackberry and apple.'

Helen was taught that when picking blackberries she must avoid belladonna. 'Deadly nightshade,' Mrs Darling used to say, in Nature Studies, holding bright berries. 'Every year some little girl or boy will die because they've eaten these, because they look nice; but they're not nice, they're poisonous, and you must keep well away.'

All morning I had listened to Alice, the cook, at work. She starts at eight o'clock each morning, boiling the kettle and tuning to Radio 2. All morning the children next door had modelled clay. Isobel is unwell with 'flu so her class had joined Mrs Whittacker's. The window blinds clinked in the breeze against the frame. Occasionally I heard Mrs Whittacker next door, her voice raised: 'Don't throw it around because it's wet, it's sticky, and if any of it ends up on the ceiling I shall be extremely cross. And take those mucky fingers out of your mouth, Kirsty Miller, you silly little girl.'

Lunch had been ready as usual by eleven o'clock. Alice stops at eleven for coffee — a teaspoon of instant and a drop of milk, a touch of sugar. She wipes the work surfaces with bleach, and then lunch is served at twelve. 'Roast,' Mr James had said enthusiastically to the group of children sitting with me at a table. He had ladled gravy over his potatoes and it slopped at the edges of his plate. He sat at the table. I wanted to ask him why Laura should have to leave her job, but I knew his reply: *Her choice, Mrs Tomlinson, in the end, isn't it. It's her choice. And women's lib may be all very well but it's just not practical, is it, Mrs Tomlinson, it's just not practical. And in an ideal world, Mrs Tomlinson, but, then, I don't need to remind you, do I, Mrs Tomlinson, that we don't live in an ideal world.*

Laura arrived back early from town. She joined me in the playground as the children were leaving.

'How was everything?' I asked her.

'Fine,' she replied.

The children were gathering at the gate, and some of them had climbed onto it.

'I haven't asked you,' I said, 'whether you have heard yet from Cassie.'

'I haven't,' she replied. 'Not yet.'

'Do you see her often?'

'Quite often.'

'Who? Who?' Harriet Lyle span towards us, breaking free from a group of mothers and children. Her own mother turned, lunged, and caught hold of her.

'Harriet!' she exclaimed, 'don't be so rude, and never mind "who".'

She smiled at us as she drew Harriet towards her. She held her with a hand on each shoulder and leaned, smiling, into her face.

'Kids,' she said, 'who'd have them?' She shook

Harriet very gently. 'This one's driving me absolutely mad today,' she said.

She straightened and relaxed her grip, patting Harriet's shoulders.

'Now go on,' she whispered loudly into her ear, 'be off with you.'

Harriet was propelled back towards the group, bumping into her brother.

'And watch where you're going,' her mother called after her as she followed.

Laura and I watched the group move away across the playground. 'Do you miss Cassie?' I asked.

'Miss her?'

'It never rains but it pours,' said Mrs Whittacker. We were standing in the cloakroom at the window. She placed a forefinger on the glass. We had been helping the children into macs and lace-ups. Mr James stood beside us.

'The British weather is supposed to be changeable,' he said, 'but I can't say I've seen much evidence of it during the past week.'

Outside, children were running towards parked cars across a grass verge, waving raincoats. Mothers followed, catching them and lifting them with coats and bags into cars before slamming doors. Dogs excitable in hatchbacks — labradors, alsatians, setters — breathed steamily against windows. Other children started out across the playground under umbrellas or under rainhats, walking together through puddles, hands held, bags swinging from shoulders.

It has rained every day for three weeks. People stop often in the streets to chat to each other about it:

*You'd never guess it was summer, would you,* they say. *Not another summer, please God, like last summer.*

Anxieties are expressed about Wimbledon. But although it rains, it remains warm. People shudder and stare into dark skies: *We're in for a storm,* they say, *and the sooner the better.*

Yesterday I found another patch of damp in John's mother's front room. 'It needs seeing to,' I told her, my finger touching the wall.

'What a nuisance,' she replied.

She was sitting in her chair. She had not been outside for days: too damp, she tells me; she worries about slipping. She sat with the cat upon her lap.

'The poor thing,' she said, stroking it, 'she hates this weather. She goes out and within minutes she's scratching at the door again to be let in.' She bent forward, rubbing its ear. 'Aren't you,' she says, 'aren't you, Tibs; you hate it, don't you, you poor old thing.'

I told her that the forecast for the weekend is better.

I don't mind the rain. I walk most evenings in the hour or so before darkness through lanes running with rainwater; the soil at the roadside soft and pressed with small stones. Occasionally cars pass me, rattling under branches, but otherwise I see no one except people in houses who are unaware of their visibility: curtains undrawn, lamps lit, lives illuminated and bright beneath glass. In the living rooms children fall within circles of lamplight onto sofas and chairs and cushions, settling to watch television. In the kitchens steam rises from colanders on draining boards and stings cool windows. I walk most evenings through the village and up the hill until I see the sky above London smarting in the distance in the dark.

This afternoon I saw Mrs Miller leaving the playground with Laura's children. Laura has been away from work: this morning Mrs Miller had brought Kirsty to school and had then spoken briefly with Mr James. At the end of the afternoon I was on my way to Mrs Whittacker's classroom when I left the building instead and followed Mrs Miller across the playground. I met her at the gate.

'Laura's unwell?'

'Under the weather.'

She waited at the gate with the pram; her hands on the handle, the little girls by her side. Several mothers passed ahead of her, nodding their thanks. The sky was overcast and she wore a coat: big, beige, buttoned across the chest. She wore on her head a headscarf printed with horseshoes and sprigs of holly.

'Hardly surprising, is it?' she said, her eyes slipping beneath their lids, 'because she hasn't been well for ages; not really. And I said she shouldn't be at work but of course she wouldn't listen.' She shrugged. The coat rose and fell. She stared absently into the pram. 'Tiredness,' she said, 'no doubt. She was never a hardy child. You'll remember, I'm sure.' She continued to stare into the pram. 'Always something wrong.' She shrugged again and stepped forward, her weight behind the pram. The wheels turned. Kirsty and Gemma moved to her side. 'And just to think,' she said, 'that there'll be another little one in four or five months' time.'

'She thinks Cassie may help her out,' I said.

Mrs Miller tilted the pram, the back wheels grinding into the gravel, the front wheels raised. She positioned it so that it would pass between the gateposts.

'Well I'd like to know why she supposes Cassie will help her out,' she said, 'because those two have absolutely nothing in common.'

On Fridays it is fish for lunch. The school smells of chips. My desk is lit by lemon sunlight, more sunlight than there has been for weeks. Laura works in the shade. She stands at the desk reading the stationery order book.

'Glad to be back?'

Her mouth closes momentarily and then opens into a small smile. She leans onto her hands, placing them wide apart on the desktop, palms flat, and drops her head; she winces as she raises it.

'Backache?'

She wrinkles her nose. 'Not too bad.'

'Doing anything nice this weekend?'

We had learned during teabreak that Isobel plans a quiet weekend at home with her husband and that next weekend they will visit Lyme Regis to stay with friends. I used to have friends in Lyme Regis. Mrs Whittacker is staying at home but will visit one of her sons for lunch on Sunday.

'Shopping,' Laura replies, 'tomorrow. With Billy. We're off to Enfield to buy a new pram.' She turns and sits on the edge of the desk, the order book in her hands.

'How will you get there?'

'By bus.'

Three buses: one to town, one to Southgate and another to Enfield.

'It's a good job your mother lives so close by.'

She resumes work, placing the order book on the desktop and sorting through the top drawer.

'The children will stay with your mother, I presume.'

'No.' Her hair falls across her face as she bends. 'They'll come with me.' She sifts papers. 'Dad's home,' she says.

'Your father's not happy to have the children around?'

'On the contrary,' she says, tucking papers into the drawer and shutting it, 'if I gave him half a chance he'd never leave them alone.'

Isobel knelt close to my desk, at the clothes cupboard, lifting garments one by one from a bag and turning with each one towards the light. Briefly she displayed a cotton dress, the shoulders pinched between her fingers, and then collapsed it over her arm. I asked her if she had recovered from her 'flu.

'Oh yes,' she said, 'thank you.' She placed the dress, folded, on a shelf and shut the cupboard door. Then she rose, biting her lip.

'Actually,' she said, after a pause, 'I've got a new job.'

So she hadn't been unwell but had been at an interview. She stood facing me, one hand on my desk. 'In St Albans,' she told me, 'just twenty or twenty-five minutes on the train; so it's much better for me and Mike, much better all round; and it's a good job, it's a nice school.'

Mrs Whittacker entered the office shortly after Isobel had left.

'Have you heard about Isobel?' she asked. She laid her register on my desk. 'What with me and you going for early retirement, and Laura and Isobel leaving,' she said, 'there'll be no one left.'

I agreed: 'What will Mr James say?' But I knew what he'd say, smiling, wincing: *These young women, you never know where you are with them, they're forever cooking something up; they're not to be trusted, coming*

*and going, here one day and gone the next; forever*
*moving on to better things, there's no stopping them*
*these days.*

Laura and I were preparing copies of the PTA AGM
agenda. Photocopies and envelopes lay in piles on the
desk. We had begun folding the copies, tucking one
into each envelope and placing it on the pile at my right
hand side or at Laura's left. A slip of paper confirming
the time and date of the Leavers' Day Church Service
was to be added later.

Mr James opened the door. 'I've been thinking,' he
said as he crossed the office towards us, 'that it would
be nice to have some extra flowers in church for the
Leavers' Day Service, but we'd need to find someone
to do them for us.'

He sat down, twisting himself onto the edge of the
desk; one foot raised, one thigh spread across the
desktop.

'Mrs Darling does the Leavers' Day flowers,' I replied, 'and she organises her own team of helpers.' I
lifted a pile of envelopes and placed them on the chair
behind me. 'The mothers are usually very willing to
help,' I continued, 'and I've had several enquiries already this term.'

'Don't tell me,' he said, leaning towards me, smirk-
ing, 'but Mrs Linton's name is the first on the list.'

Laura's hands faltered.

'From what I hear,' he continued, snickering, 'her
garden runneth over, so we can be certain that there
will be no shortage of flowers.'

Laura's hands remained above the photocopies:
motionless, empty, clean.

I reached for another photocopy. 'Mrs Linton is one of our most willing helpers,' I said.

'Yes,' he said. He straightened. 'Of course.'

I turned to Laura and smiled. I handed her some envelopes from the box on the floor at my side. She smiled back.

Mr James sighed. 'So the flower arranging can be left to Mrs Darling?'

'It is best to ask her,' I replied.

'I'll leave it with you to check,' he said. 'And the vicar tells me that it's his responsibility to organise the giving of a gift each year from the Governors to the leavers.'

'Yes,' I said. We had resumed folding.

'Prayer books, I believe,' he said.

'Yes,' I said, 'or sometimes a dictionary.'

'Prayer books this year,' he said, swinging his legs so that his feet reached the floor. He stood. 'Flowers . . . gifts . . . is there anything else?'

'The photograph.'

'The photograph,' He stared at me.

I reached to the back of my chair for my cardigan. 'We have a photograph taken on Leavers' Day every year,' I told him.

'But can't the parents take their own photographs?'

'No,' I said, dropping the cardigan across my shoulders, 'they can't. Many of them can't be here, and many of them don't have cameras.'

'Well in that case I suppose we had better set about engaging the services of a professional photographer.'

'Mr Bennett has confirmed,' I said.

'Mr Bennett?'

'He comes every year. Sophie Bennett's grandfather' — I turned to Laura — 'and Elizabeth Grant's father-in-law?'

She nodded. 'Yes,' she replied. 'Lizzie Grant; Lizzie Bennett.'

I turned back to Mr James. 'He has a studio on the High Street. He took most of the photographs lining the wall behind your desk.'

'The school photographs?' Mr James lifted a copy of the agenda from the pile on the desk and glanced at it.

'Taken on Leavers' Days.'

He continued reading. 'So everyone is present for the photograph,' he asked, 'not just the leavers?' He dropped the agenda onto the desk.

'They all go to the Service, don't they,' I replied, 'so they all sit for the photograph, and they all come to the party.' I replaced the agenda on the appropriate pile.

'Party?'

'Party.' Coconut ice pressed pink and white into baking tins, chocolate Rice Crispy cakes spooned into paper cases, and peppermint cream daubed onto greaseproof paper; parcels passed, slipped around the circle; and games, make-believe, pretending, amber limbs in long grass and summer clothes brilliant through the blades.

'Party?' he said, 'Who is in charge of this party?'

'In charge?'

He stood with his feet apart, clutching a sheaf of papers to his chest.

'Who is in charge of the food, for instance?'

'Anna, the cook, of course,' I said.

Laura lifted a sheet from the top of the pile and began to fold it. Mr James leaned across the desk and laid a hand on her arm.

'Laura,' he said, 'can I ask you, before I forget, to take these papers along to my room? They should be seen to this afternoon so you might like to drop them into my tray.'

She nodded and he handed her the papers and waited until she had left the room before speaking.

'I trust,' he said to me when she had left, 'that everyone will be ship-shape on the day? Mr Hardy — Chairman of the Governors — is attending the service and I regard it as essential that everyone is presentable and on best behaviour.'

I reached across the desk for Laura's completed envelopes. 'They will be,' I said, 'because they have their party and the photograph to look forward to.'


Laura told me later that afternoon of her next clinic appointment.

'So soon?'

She was breathless, she claimed; and lethargic. She wanted a check-up; it could be a lack of iron.

She was sitting hunched on a chair pulled away from the desk; her forearms on her thighs, her stomach sagging with skirt between her knees. On her ankle veins faintly visible blew beneath the surface of the skin.

'I haven't felt well for ages,' she said.

'No.'

Her head dropped. 'Tiredness, I suppose.'

'Perhaps.'

Spangles of sunlight nestled in her hair.

'You are very pale,' I said.

She looked up at me and blinked. She rubbed her eyes. 'Actually,' she said, 'I'm hot.' She looked at the window. It was open.

'Clammy,' I said.

She lifted herself out of the chair and walked slowly across the room to the window. She laid her fingertips on the sill. 'Anxiety,' she said, 'that's what the doctor said.'

'Three children and a job,' I replied, 'is a lot for anyone to cope with.'

'Four children,' she said, fingertips tapping. She turned, struck by sunlight before she shielded herself. She winced and raised a hand to her eyes. 'I do my best,' she said. Her eyes blistered and watered.

'Yes.'

'My mother said I shouldn't have another.'

'I know.'

I stepped towards her. Above the window behind her there was a blind which could be unrolled.

'People say I don't care for my children,' she said, 'but I do.'

She watched me as I felt for the strings.

'Who says that?'

The blind fell against the glass.

'I do care,' she said, 'I do.'

I steadied the blind with my hands before returning to my desk. Laura remained at the window. She did not move.

'I know you do,' I said.

She stood with her arms at her sides. 'My father said I shouldn't have this baby — did you know that?' Still she did not move.

'Abortion?'

'But this child is mine.' She folded her hands in front of her. 'Mine,' she said again, 'mine.'

Several years ago I visited the doctor for a routine check-up. I discovered when I arrived that my doctor was on holiday, and that I had an appointment with a locum.

'Hop up onto the couch,' he said to me after introducing himself. He glanced through my records.

The couch was at the side of the room: high, narrow, leather, with a pillow at one end and a blanket folded at the other. Across the middle the doctor had placed a sheet of paper, newly unfolded and plastic-backed.

'Hop up here,' he said, 'and slip your panties off.'

I lay on the couch, my knees bent and parted. The doctor stood by my feet, his white coat not so white, his pockets cluttered with torch and scissors and pencils and pens. He placed his right hand inside a plastic glove, and bent between my legs. He probed with a finger.

'I'm just going to. . .'

He reached behind him and lifted a speculum from a tray on the table. He held it momentarily in both hands, fixing it before sliding it inside me. Bending again between my legs, he glanced up at me and smiled. 'A bit cold, I expect,' he said.

He bent lower, shifting his feet: 'Let's have a little look.' He frowned. 'How many pregnancies have you had, Mrs Tomlinson?'

'One,' I told him. 'A little girl, Helen.'

'Right,' he said, leaning, squinting, his hands at work. 'And now,' he said, 'I'll take just a few cells from the cervix, for the microscope.' He cut; and the speculum slid away. 'All done,' he said, straightening and smiling, 'and not too bad after all, eh?'

He returned to his desk, sitting and reaching for a pile of cards — medical records, my medical records slipped from their envelope, stacked flat, well thumbed. He began writing on the uppermost, scratching across the matt surface with his nib whilst delving with his other hand amongst the remaining cards, sifting them through his fingers and glancing at them from time to time. I sat with my skirt pulled to my knees. Eventually he paused and read one of the cards, frowning.

'Two,' he said, 'you've had two pregnancies.' He replaced it on the pile.

'It came away at five months,' I said.

He had resumed writing. 'It was female,' he said, 'did anyone tell you?'

Miscarriage: *spontaneous abortion* they call it; *not a nice word*, the doctor had sympathised. *It happens, Mrs Tomlinson, it happens,* he had said; *it's nature's way, Mrs Tomlinson, try to think of it as nature's way; and it's for the best, Mrs Tomlinson, believe me — no damage, nothing permanent, nothing wrong, nothing to worry about, nothing whatsoever, and you're young, Mrs Tomlinson, you're fit and healthy, and I suggest you go home and try to forget about it and try again soon for another.*

I returned home after a few days in hospital and everything had been the same as when I left: it was late summer and Helen played outside every day until dusk, knowing not to go far and to return for her tea. Summer became winter and she played less, her days ending at four o'clock with her return from school. Kicking off her shoes at the foot of the stairs, she'd enter the living room and switch on the television and flick through the channels, impatient with the test card.

Homework, I'd remind her. And tidy away your shoes.

In a minute, she'd reply.

She would come into the kitchen and reach inside the breadbin.

Leave some for breakfast, I'd say as I watched her tearing at the loaf with a breadknife.

I don't eat breakfast, she'd reply.

You *do*, I'd say; and, anyway, *I* do.

And who cares about *you*, she'd say, grinning and popping another piece into her mouth.

At other times she raided the biscuit tin or lifted hot scones from the cooling rack.

'They're hot, they'll give you wind,' I told her each time, 'and please leave some for your father.'

She always reached for another. 'What the eye doesn't see. . .'

*'Helen. . .'*

'Only kidding.'

Sometimes in the evenings she sat at the table whilst I cooked, or stood at the cooker stirring the gravy as it simmered. She chattered on these evenings about her classes and teachers — the ones she didn't like, and the ones she did, and why. She leaned across the table as I served and dipped into saucepans, sometimes with a fork, sometimes with fingers: *A little more of this, please, a little less of that; just a little then, just a fraction, just a taste; and no peas, please.*

We used to eat at six o'clock, or at half past. She refused liver, always, but liked fish. Best of all she liked tinned plums, Victoria plums, in syrup with custard so hot that it burned the roof of her mouth.

John returned home late in the evenings; hanging up his coat and sitting at the table with the newspaper. I'd fetch his food — warm still, in the oven, and covered but dry. He'd add sauce from a bottle, mashing it into the potato. Pudding followed, a portion set aside in a bowl.

When she was older Helen sat in the evenings in the dining room with her homework. She sat in lamplight, her head bowed, her chin in her hands, the leather elbow patches of her blazer worn thin. Sometimes she sat curled around the phone at the foot of the stairs, the cord wire stretched across the hall; sitting away from draughts, huddling close to the radiator; the receiver at her ear, her head inclined, her eyes watchful, her voice low.

I offered to take care of Laura's children after school once again while she attended the antenatal clinic, but Mrs Miller called at the house shortly after I arrived.

'It's only right, isn't it,' she insisted, 'that a man should take an interest in his own grandchildren.' She stepped up onto the doorstep and laid a hand on the door frame. 'He takes an interest, that's all,' she said.

Behind me in the living room at the end of the hallway Kirsty and Gemma watched television.

'What's the use of all this upsetting people?' Mrs Miller continued. The ends of her headscarf lifted in the breeze.

'I'm only telling you what she said,' I told her.

She nodded. 'I know,' she said, 'and I appreciate what you're doing, Mrs Tomlinson, but it'll be a lot easier for everyone if the children stay at my house until Laura gets back. It'll be a lot less trouble.'

I stepped back into the hallway. She stepped forward so that the door would not close. Her face was in darkness. 'She's a silly girl,' she said, 'and she says some silly things. Cassie was my husband's favourite and Laura is an unforgiving little soul, if you ask me, an envious little girl, vindictive, manipulative.'

Lines ran in the shadows around her mouth. 'Why is she doing this?' she wailed as I closed the door, 'what good will it do?'

'I don't know,' I said, 'but I'm telling you what she told me: under no circumstances while I am taking care of her children should her father be allowed access to them.'

I have been in the garden all day. It is good weather for getting things done. It is Sunday, and in the houses all around there has been cooking from mid-morning until late afternoon: meat and poultry trussed and spitting in tins, vegetables diced and steamed, plates warmed and places set. In the garden it is hot still; but hotter still indoors, sunlight sifting through the rooms. I am sitting on the lawn. Next door, on the other side of the fence, Josephine plays ball. She has played all afternoon, waiting for lunch, listening to the radio; humming along to *Jimmy Savile*, waiting for the *Top 40*. On one occasion the ball landed in my flowerbed.

'Josephine,' her mother called as I handed it back, 'say thank you to Mrs Tomlinson.'

'Thank you Mrs Tomlinson.'

Josephine attends a prep school — a convent — dressed in boater, blazer and tunic. She carries a briefcase, hockey stick, or cake tin. Her mother is a travel agent and her father a policeman.

'Having a nice day?' her mother called to me.

'Yes, very nice, thank you,' I replied.

Later I heard her calling to other neighbours over other fences: 'What a lovely day we're having; aren't we lucky.'

Across the gardens at the back of my house is the village hall: two-storey, redbrick, net curtains at the caretaker's window. Until twelve years ago there was no kitchen at the school and the children walked instead at lunchtime behind their teacher across the village to the village hall. It was rebuilt several years ago with a stage, a committee room, a kitchen, two cloakrooms, a car park and a first floor caretaker's flat. On Saturday evenings throughout each summer it hosts wedding receptions.

'I have exams on Monday,' Helen used to mutter, irritable, anxious to sleep but woken at midnight by revellers in the car park, or awake perhaps throughout. Mrs Spraggon is caretaker. Mrs Dragon, Helen used to call her: *Dragon, Dragon-breath, Dragon-face, Puff.* Helen went weekly to Youth Club at the hall and Mrs Spraggon was not fond of youths: 'Noisy little blighters,' she would shout down the stairs at them, 'make sure the chairs are back where you found them.'

Helen sat here every day during late summer ten years ago. She faced out across the gardens.

'You'd better come in,' I would tell her at the end of each day.

I had written to her form mistress: *You will be aware, no doubt, that Helen has had a difficult time lately, and I would be grateful for your understanding.*

Mr James stood in the office doorway with papers in his arms. Flickering in the corridor behind him

were children on their way to the playground. There
are a few mistakes in this morning's letters, he told
me, and I wonder if you'd mind very much re-typing
them?

He licked the index finger of his free hand and
applied it to the papers, whipping through them and
making the pile fluffy. Mrs Whittacker crossed the
corridor behind him, tapping her teeth with a biro.
She smiled at me as she passed: Mistakes, she said to
me over his shoulder, tut tut, you're getting old, losing
your touch.

Mr James drew several sheets from the pile, stepped
forwards and placed them on my desk. I leafed through
them as he left: '40' instead of '14'; 'dyslectic' instead of
'dyslexic'; and, added in pencil to Mr Hardy's letter, his
best wishes to Mrs Hardy.

When we turned from the window that day, from the
rain, from the mothers and children hand-in-hand in
the playground, it was Laura whom we watched. The
last of the mothers in the cloakroom, she knelt in front
of her little girl, dressing her in a coat. Mr James
talked about rain on St Swithin's day whilst Laura
moved the little girl into the coat, moving arms into
sleeves. Mittens dangled on string for safekeeping.
Laura's fingertips brushed collar and cuffs but she
gazed into the face of her daughter and the little
girl gazed back. They whispered together about buttons — top buttons, missing buttons — and about
hometime, teatime, teatime treats, and I don't know
what, I couldn't hear. But I saw that day how Laura's
children are her salvation. I also saw how she has been
subject throughout her life to scrutiny and supervision
and has always hated it.

There had been no word from Cassie.

Laura was sitting on the desk, having left Gemma a few moments earlier with Isobel. She smiled, shrugged, her shoulders twitching beneath her pale yellow cardigan. The smile was bright. She wore a hairband of a similar shade to the cardigan; uncovered, her forehead gleamed. Her legs were swinging, crossed at the ankle, one heel knocking repeatedly against wood.

'Anything would do,' I said, 'any word about what she's planning to do, any word about what you might expect from her.'

I had returned to the office with the post; I stood sorting envelopes in the doorway.

'She's busy, I expect,' replied Laura.

I dropped some of the letters into the filing tray.

'She could so easily put your mind at rest.'

'She has her own life to lead.' Laura's feet swung to the floor.

'You need to know whether or not she is coming over to help you,' I continued, 'and when, and for how long.'

I placed some papers in the bulldog clip on the noticeboard. When I turned, Laura was standing: she stood in front of the desk, her feet together, her hands behind her back, the edge of the desk top between her fingertips. The light from the window was motionless in each of her eyes, the panes reflected.

She told me quietly that the children would have to go to Cassie in Reading because Cassie would never return to the village; and that she, Laura, had never expected it to be otherwise; and why, she asked, was I so worried about it?

I crossed the room towards her: 'Because something needs to be said.'

My reflection loomed across the surface of her eyes.

Suddenly I understood how Laura was requesting no more than she was due by asking for Cassie's help. The most obvious explanation for Laura's attention seeking had been her envy of Cassie but it wasn't true because she had never envied Cassie. She had no cause to envy Cassie: Cassie dazzled, she turned heads, but heads once turned will turn again. What had I remembered about her apart from the hair, the smile, the fingernails? And I had seen how Laura had hated attention, how she had cringed from it. I had seen that she would never have sought attention, not for herself, and that if her life had been one long cry for help then it had been on behalf of someone else. It had been on behalf of Cassie. It had been an inadequate response to an intolerable situation.

'People assumed that you envied Cassie.'

Laura shrugged. 'She was my father's favourite.' She spoke very quietly, my reflection still in her eyes.

'I know,' I said, 'and it wasn't easy for her.'

Laura turned away. I followed her to the window.

'There was an expression for it in my day,' I told her. 'Unwelcome attentions.'

Mrs Whittacker asked me whether I had heard the news. She had called in at the office on her way home to ask me about the collection for Isobel. She spoke from the doorway.

The news, she said, is that the little Polish boy is dying: no more remission.

Children die in accidents, I thought as she turned away. Not of cancer, surely, not like adults sick and dying sweaty in pyjamas; not these days, surely. Children run across roads, I thought, and that is how they die: *Here one minute and gone the next.*

*Hold my hand,* I used to say to Helen, *and stay by my side: left, right and left again.*

I remembered as Mrs Whittacker closed the door behind her that there are other ways for children to die: they slip away before dawn, *all right one minute and gone the next;* passing like a shudder through others' lives and leaving photos in albums and rusks in the cupboard and dummies and nappies and where on earth do you keep a dead baby's things? Helen slept throughout her childhood on smother-proof pillows.

Babies bounce, Mrs Tomlinson, said the doctor. But to be on the safe side I fitted stairgates and fireguards; and I sterilized utensils, and washed, stewed, and strained all of her food.

He is dying, Mrs Whittacker had said.

She imagines the gentle swish of curtains around his bed. She forgets that he has had a lifetime of dying; that he will not remember a time when doctors and nurses have not circled his bed, detectable in darkness solely by the rattle of their charts. Until he dies his temperature will be taken every fifteen minutes; and his eyelids lifted, his pupils sliced by torchbeam.

Before leaving hospital ten years ago for the last time John lay for days with a tube in his nose; his breathing blunt, his words slow.

'Can't he come home?' I asked the staff.

'We know it's distressing to watch, Mrs Tomlinson,' the doctor replied, 'but medicine is compromise, not miracle.'

'We do our best,' the nurse explained. 'The tube

drains the stomach to remove the fluid and he'll feel
better in the end.'

There is no such thing as a good death.

'Why don't you come home now?' I asked John when
the tube had been removed.

'Won't it be difficult?' he asked me.

'No,' I said, 'not for long.'

At home after each outpatient treatment he was
sicker.

Turn the telly down, Helen, I'd say, or the record;
and be quiet on the stairs; and, Helen, please, no more
friends around.

Oh let her, he'd say to me. Let her be.

In the early summer ten years ago he sat for hours
each day in the garden. He sat in a straight-backed
dining chair, facing away; and although he smiled
whenever I approached, I knew what he ached to say:
that if the treatment was this bad then he would rather
die. He knew people would reply that he was a lucky
man, luckier than he knew, lucky to be alive.

Throughout the summer the doctors were cruel to be
kind, administering chemotherapy; the needle deep,
the drug washed into the bloodstream before it could
burn. They wore gloves to protect themselves from
spillage. People told me that John was brave, but
he endured because he had no choice: cytotoxins are
— literally — cell poisoners, and he was poisoned
in the hope that the cancer would die first but it
didn't.


No, Helen had said when I had visited her at her flat,
there was nothing I could do.

She continued to slice bread. The last of the

afternoon sun was on her shoulders, her bones bright beneath her skin. As she sliced, her fingertips pressed into the loaf. She has my mother's hands; my mother's hands as I remember them cool and slender in linen, in tea towels and sheets or the folds of her skirts. Behind Helen the curtains billowed with the noise from the street; increasing throughout the afternoon and evening with the return of schoolchildren and workers to the neighbourhood.

'I don't know how you manage to live in London,' I remarked.

She laid the bread knife down and glanced at me as she reached across the worktop for the bowl of salad.

'You should have avoided the West End,' she said, 'and, anyway, you used to manage it.'

She shook the lettuce leaves from the bowl and laid them on the slices of bread.

'Not by choice,' I reminded her. 'When I last lived in London I was a child.'

'But you miss it.' She pressed slices of bread onto the lettuce leaves.

'Not by choice,' I said.

She cut the bread diagonally and arranged the sandwiches on a plate. For her Brownie Hostess Badge she had learned to arrange sandwiches with doilies and sprigs of parsley.

'You were always such a capable child,' I remembered.

'No, I wasn't,' she said. She lifted the plate from the worktop and came towards me.

'Yes, you were,' I said.

'No, I wasn't.'

'Yes, Helen,' I said, reaching and taking the plate from her hand, 'yes you were.'

'No,' she said, 'I wasn't. And, anyway,' she said as she turned away, 'how would you have ever known.'

Now I remember how she had appeared at the kitchen door one night ten years ago; in pyjamas, her hair newly washed and rubbed in handfuls and left tumbling towel-dry to her shoulders.

'Helen,' I said from where I sat reading the paper, 'it's late.'

'I know,' she replied. Her hands were flat at either side of her on the doorframe. 'It's Dad,' she said. 'He wants me to talk to him.'

Her hands began to move at either side of her across the wood. 'Talk to me, he says, stay, talk to me, and eventually, he says, I'll sleep; but he won't, he lies awake, he is lying awake up there now and what more can I say to him?'

'He'll sleep,' I said.

'No,' she said, 'he won't.'

'Helen,' I said, 'you're tired.'

She crossed her arms in front of her chest, and her hands gripped her shoulders.

'He wants me to talk,' she said, 'but what can I say?'

'Anything,' I told her, 'any old thing, it doesn't matter.'

Her arms shook inside pink nylon sleeves.

'When I was small,' she said, 'he used to sit with me at night and tell me stories until I slept.'

'You were a sensible child,' I said. 'You didn't believe in stories.'

'But I believed in *him*.'

'Helen,' I said, 'it's very late and you should be in bed.'

'I used to tell him everything,' she said, 'but not now.'

'And dry your hair,' I said, 'or you'll catch a cold.'

'Now I tell him nothing because there's nothing to tell,' she said.

'Helen.'

'What have you done today, he asks; tell me what you've done, tell me what you've seen, what you've learned, tell me everything.'

Her arms were suddenly unfolded.

'Helen.'

'Nothing.' Her hands were in front of her again; and at her sides, the door, the door frame, the door handle, at her head, her hair. 'Nothing,' she said, 'nothing, I do nothing but wait for him to die.'

'Helen,' I said, 'please.'

'I want him to know,' she said.

'Helen, no.'

'Tell him,' she said, 'please tell him, Mum, that he's dying.'

'No,' I said.

'Mum, please.'

'No.'

'Tell him,' she said, turning, her wrists and ankles slipping beneath her pyjamas, 'tell him; because if you won't, I will.'

And then what did I say to her: that she wouldn't dare? Did I? Did I tell her that she wasn't to open her mouth, that she wasn't to breathe a word? Did I? And that if she did I'd kill her? Did I say those things to her? And the rest? Did I tell her how I wished John and I could have time together alone; time like we had had in the beginning, in the days before she was born? Or did I simply tell her to go upstairs and leave me alone; because that, in the end, was what she did.

In the end I don't think John ever knew. I don't think Helen ever told him. In the end he moved into the spare room because it was quieter. I remember how he vomited one afternoon, missing the bowl, and apologised when I lifted his head to remove the pillow.

'Don't be silly,' I told him.

It had been a sunless afternoon, the sky sheer above the trees and blank between the branches.

'What time is it? he asked.

'I don't know,' I replied.

The clock, which ticked noisily, had been moved from the chest of drawers to the hallway and I had replaced it with a bowl of pot pourri from the dressing table.

'It's late,' I said.

The older children had returned hours beforehand from secondary school.

'It seems to darken earlier these days,' he said.

I drew the curtains, shaking loose the folds. 'Trust me,' I said.

He did; he trusted me. He had no choice. People told me afterwards that there was nothing more I could have done but the fact remains that he trusted me with his life and I lost it.


John's mother sat in the straight-backed armchair at the fireplace, her feet side by side in slippers on the tiled hearth. It is a gas fire and remained unlit today as on all other summer days. I had called in to see if there was anything she wanted.

She asked me to wait with her because a man would be calling later about the damp. She asked me to sit, and she made tea, bringing it on a tray and placing it on the coffee table in the middle of the room between us. She sat back in her armchair and smiled at me. 'You're on your way home from swimming.'

I touched the ends of my hair; they were damp. 'Yes,' I said.

'Swimming is an excellent form of exercise, isn't it?' she said. She raised her hands slowly from her lap and examined them. They were stiff with arthritis. 'Swimming keeps everything moving, doesn't it.' She dropped them back into her lap. 'Everything is much easier in water than on land.'

The pendulum of the mantelpiece clock swung through the seconds.

She sighed. 'You were so very active when you were a girl. I remember how you stayed here with us at weekends before you were married: you'd be up and out before either of us had woken, and I'd see you later in the distance in the fields or in the lane, collecting flowers or berries or grasses; and I'd say to John, look, there she is over there, in the field or in the lane. And after you were married you played tennis, didn't you. You were very good at tennis.'

I poured the tea and handed her a cup. She smiled her thanks.

'And table tennis, too,' she continued, 'and hockey, and the classes in the evenings — dressmaking, curtain making, rugs, history — do you remember the rug you made for me? I still have it, the blue one, upstairs in the hallway.'

She sipped at her tea. 'And then Helen was born,' she said, placing the cup and saucer on the arm of the chair, 'and you'd bring her in to see me on your way back from town in all weathers with library books and shopping.'

I handed her the plate of biscuits but she declined and I replaced it on the tray.

'And then,' she said, 'there were the expeditions to London when you'd drag your shopping bags around the shops and on and off the trains and buses all day on your own.' She lifted the cup and saucer. 'I used to ask John how he had ever thought that he would keep up with you.'

We sipped in silence.

'Helen's the same,' I said eventually. 'Helen loved swimming, didn't she?'

'Helen isn't looking after herself.' The cup and saucer were balanced in her lap.

I placed my cup and saucer on the tray and reached behind me for my jacket. I lifted it from the back of my chair. 'Mum,' I said, 'Helen isn't a child anymore.'

'She's starving herself,' she replied, edging forwards in her seat. 'She is starving herself, and don't tell me that you hadn't noticed the bones clean through her clothes.'

I looked up at the clock. It was a few minutes after five o'clock; the man would not now be calling about the damp. 'If that's what she wants to do,' I said as I stood, 'then there's absolutely nothing I can do about it, is there.'

## SCAN

You lie on a table and they spread cold jelly over your stomach; then a woman comes and sits beside you and slides a bleeper across it. Attached to the bleeper is a machine with a screen at which the woman smiles and points.

'Look,' she says, 'there's the baby — see? — the head, and the spine.' On the screen something swells in darkness and turns and sinks. As I lay waiting I heard nurses and radiographers asking questions of their patients: 'Have you decided on a name?' 'Do you want a boy or a girl?' The woman in the cubicle next to mine told them that it didn't matter as long as the baby was healthy.

I heard the nurses laughing: 'Healthy? This little one will be playing football for England in a few years time, you mark my words.' But now, now that it is my turn, no one is laughing. A woman slides a bleeper across my stomach. She stares at the screen; I stare at the ceiling. Eventually she switches off the machine, and rises from her seat. 'That's all,' she says.

She asks me not to forget my next appointment with the doctor, and then she leaves the room.

I changed back into my clothes, and caught the bus home. The sky was mottled with cloud but the streets were hot and dry. I walked from the bus-stop at the shopping arcade towards my house. In gardens behind fences transistor radios sang lunchtime radio shows: DJs chatted, quizzed, and chanted their telephone numbers: *Get your feet up, girls, and put the kettle on, and here's a mention for all of you in the office* ... Their voices came too from inside cars parked at the roadside; cars with windows dropped, doors opened, occupants leaving pastries or sandwiches on the dashboard and heading for the newsagent. When I arrived home Jenny wasn't there. Sometimes she stays at college over lunchtime. Next week she will be away on holiday in Corfu with her boyfriend.

She's a young woman now, my husband says, and we can't tell her what she can and can't do.

He will not be here until Thursday. He was promoted recently at work and is required now to spend a few nights away from home each week. I have not yet grown used to it. I had expected to have a little more time with him, not less, as we grew older.

It is hot. The house smells of furniture polish. I opened the door to the garden. Outside it is not yet dark. We lived until recently in the north; and in the north during the summer the sky doesn't blacken at night but flames a deeper blue and melts the sun. The sky in the south is black and sweet at night like chocolate.

Jenny is in the bathroom indulging in rituals behind a closed door. She will emerge cleansed and shaved and deodorised; toned, conditioned, and moisturised; her hair wrapped around her head in a towel. She had always been a grubby child, leaving tidemarks around the bath, and I had to bathe her every evening during the summer. She would have grass stains on her knees and soil under her nails. She used to look dirty however hard I scrubbed. She has sallow skin. After her bath each evening I would tuck her into her bed, smoothing the sheets around her skinny limbs; her brown wrists and ankles sticking out of the Mickey Mouse pyjamas or Mr Men nightshirt or whatever else she had chosen the last time we had been to the big stores. When she slept, her hair pressed against the pillow smelled of sweet sweat. Jenny never makes mistakes: there are packets of pretty pink pills in the drawer by her bed.

This morning, before leaving for the hospital, I vomited. I flushed the toilet and dowsed it with bleach but then I vomited again. The vomit slid in streaks down the sides of the bowl. I have been sick every morning for the past three months.

Gastro-enteritis, the doctor said initially, a bug, a virus; and then he had explained the irregular bleeding as a result of my stopping taking the pill.

'Things will take time to settle down,' he said.

Pregnancy is the latest of his explanations and as yet I remain unconvinced. I am bleeding still every month, and I never bled when pregnant with Jenny. I never vomited either.

'Things change,' the doctor said when I told him, 'and all that was a long time ago.'

It was a very long time ago. I told him that I was too old to have another baby.

'Not at all,' he said, 'lots of women have babies

when, like you, they are in their late thirties; in fact, lots of women *start* to have babies when they are in their late thirties.'

I started when I was eighteen.


I went shopping with Jenny for maternity clothes. They aren't so hideous these days, she claimed, and there are Young Mum departments in most of the shops. But this mum isn't so young anymore.

'Very neat,' the shop assistants said, 'very becoming.'

I was forced to parade in front of mirrors: mirrors in front and mirrors behind.

One of the assistants asked if Jenny and I were sisters.

'You look alike,' she said.

My mother always believed that people were thinkers or doers. Jenny is a doer but I am a thinker. I watched breathless as Jenny scraped through childhood. She mastered all the steps as if they were songs or nursery rhymes, as if she could perform them back to front or standing on her head if she wanted; they have remained with her ever since as snippets hummed from time to time.

People say that children learn by imitation, but Jenny exhibited a precision in her development which belied any haphazard collecting of facts. She understood what made things tick. She was a clever child with clever hands, taking hold of things and taking them apart, unfolding her hands and revealing: *Here's a church, here's a steeple*. But she was a thinker, too, in many ways; and she is a thinker still, in many ways, and perhaps more than ever now that she can no longer hop, skip and jump. She was a formidable thinker because she knew exactly what she wanted. She worked through every consequence and complication; she calculated; and all that I ever saw was her winning smile. Her childhood has disappeared in a blur of handstands and cartwheels pasted into photo albums. I feel that I have left no mark upon her. She could have been someone else's child. But she is her father's daughter; and he telephoned us this evening after we had come back from shopping but didn't speak for long as he didn't have much to say.

Today I have been sick all day. I have been in bed. At teatime Jenny tried to make me eat something but I asked her instead for a drink. She brought me iced tea with fruit on top and chunks of ice floating below. When left alone I hear sounds from my silenced radio. Yesterday I mentioned it to my husband when he telephoned.

'It hisses,' I said.

'It buzzes,' he told me; 'and it has always buzzed; and if you're worried, you could unplug it.'

Today I did not speak to him. He telephoned earlier but Jenny answered and told him that I was unwell and should not be disturbed.

At dusk today I became aware of Jenny at the foot of my bed. I lay still under the sheet and eventually she moved across the room to the window and drew the curtains. When she left I rose and sat on the edge of the bed, listening for familiar sounds. I listened for the Toddler Group mums wheeling their prams along the street, and for the children playing rounders on the green, but I was too late; everyone had gone indoors for the evening. Someone somewhere was washing a car, slopping a sponge around a bucket. It was the only sound. There was nothing else.

I slept for several hours and now I am lying in bed feeling with my fingertips the pulse swelling in my neck. I am sluggish, heavy, constipated, and the baby is still. It has never moved. I have never felt it move. Jenny, however, moves below me downstairs in darkness. She should have gone to bed long ago. She moves slowly from room to room and then she moves back again, retracing her steps. Occasionally she trips and clatters and curses. I should have reminded her to lock the doors and windows because often she forgets. She forgets to unplug the switches too, and one day there will be a fire.

Today Jenny is peculiarly painted. She has told me that she will be going out later this evening, but for now she sits in the kitchen with her father. He returned home earlier this evening. They sit together at the kitchen table in their bathrobes. She crosses her legs, and her big toe brushes against the hairs on his leg. When younger she sat for hours with my mother-in-law. The gigantic old lady had been wedged into a wheelchair and covered with blankets; and Jenny clambered into her lap so that with yellowing hands the old lady could stroke her granddaughter's darkly tangled hair. Jenny captivated even then with her mixture of swagger and vulnerability, and for hours the old lady was quietened and would sit smoothing Jenny's hair, gobbling and spitting her twisted tales and half-digested truths.

They never wanted this baby, Jenny and her father; and babies know when they aren't wanted. They can sense a bad atmosphere. This baby has never moved; I have not eaten for several days; I do not want to grow any larger. My stomach, empty, swells only temporarily. I haven't long to wait now for the results of the scan; the hospital appointment card is balanced on the mantelpiece. This afternoon I sat for a while on the doorstep. Next door there was a paddling pool spread across the lawn. Sunlight reflected on the water. At sunset clouds lay on the horizon like peach slices. My husband will not be home until tomorrow. I sat on the doorstep and watched the neighbours returning from work. I watched them driving their cars into garages and I listened to them switching off engines and slamming doors. In their houses lamplight sprang in spheres against closed curtains and dropped later into darkness.

Throughout the evening Jenny moved backwards and forwards from room to room across the hall behind me. Once she approached me and placed her fingertips on my scalp before dropping a cardigan into my lap.

'Keep warm,' she said.

Then, later, she brought me a herbal concoction in a teapot.

'Drink it,' she said, 'it'll do you good.'

I placed it beside me on the doorstep.

She shrugged. 'It won't do you any harm,' she said. They were the very words that her grandmother had used many years ago. It was as if she had repeated them, as if she had remembered them; yet she couldn't have remembered them because they had been said before she had been born. I had been pregnant, my skirt stretched tight across my stomach, and the old woman had assumed that her son would not wish to marry me but had smiled nonetheless when introduced. She had smiled in a manner considered appropriate for a woman of her social standing. She told me as soon as we had been left alone together that her son was too young to have a child. 'So you might like to drink this,' she said. She handed me a glass of sweet smelling herbal tea. 'It won't do you any harm,' she said.

And neither did it work.

So in the end the old lady had passed her secrets to Jenny. Jenny is good at keeping secrets. Trustworthy, it used to say on her school reports. Secretive, perhaps. I had waited until I was alone again on the doorstep before tipping the sweet smelling liquid from the teapot to the soil at my feet. Then, eventually, I came into the house. At first we sat here for several hours, Jenny and I, in the living room. She sat opposite me in an armchair. She pretended to read the newspaper. Sometimes her eyes darted towards me, pale and moist and globular like round-bellied fish. Shortly before the rain began she rose to close the window; and soon afterwards, a few minutes before midnight, she told me that she was going to bed. She rose for a second time, folded the newspaper and dropped it into the armchair before leaving. Jenny is secretive: she has a store of secrets,

a secret store, because where else are all her hurts
and disappointments? On her face there is only that
winning smile. She knows so many things, so many,
many things about me; she has lived with me for so
many years. Traces of her remain here in the room
with me: the newspaper, folded; the face powder
fallen onto the rug; the pencil slipped among the
sofa cushions. Rain slithers across the roof. On the
sideboard the pot plants cast no shadow or shade.
Despite her smile, her painted smile, my mother-
in-law had been a wicked witch with wicked secrets;
and now I realize that Jenny has not escaped: I see
streaks of it, that wickedness, in my own flesh and
blood. But I know what to do about witches, I know
how to be free of spells: I must burn everything of
mine that she has ever possessed. So what I must do
is strike a match and drop it, here, now; and it will be
a long time on a night like this before anyone comes
running and shouting and trying to discover if there
is anyone left inside.

# SISTERS

The Snow Queen had returned. Mum says I shouldn't call her that because it isn't nice and because she's my sister. But it's so apt that I can't resist it; and, anyway, she's not my sister, not really. She's mum's daughter. I went along when mum drove into town to fetch her from the station. The streets were quieter than usual, emptier. It was mid-afternoon, the sun jabbing between the leaves of the trees and slapping onto the bodywork of the cars in front. I sat straight, trying to level my eyes with the sunstrip on our windscreen but I didn't have much luck and ended up squinting as usual. If it hadn't been August, if it hadn't been school holiday time then the kids would have been coming out of the primary school. But the afternoon was empty. Nobody hurried along to the wine bar for a sandwich or nipped into the Co-op for a tin of beans or a loaf of sliced white. Those who went out to work were still there, behind plate glass, watching the clock. Those at home groped behind net curtains to open their windows wider. Everyone was waiting but the evening was still hours away. The cars weren't yet

queueing to leave the station car park; it wasn't yet
time for the News or the evening meal, nor time to
bath the kiddies, nor frying time, nor opening time.

We drove along the High Street past the school.
The gates were closed and padlocked, a bolt driven
into the asphalt. There were no children trailing
cardigans in the dust or playing chase or clinging
to pushchairs. There were no young mums to sal-
vage mucky cardigans and stuff them into shopping
bags or over pushchair handles; no parked cars with
stickers warning you about deaf children or asking
you to support the teachers; no satchels, discarded,
hanging on railings, bulging with plimsolls and
today's letter home thanking and reminding and
adding a note of caution. Even the lollipop lady
had deserted her post. No doubt she was at home,
quite unrecognisable. But down some streets I saw
children riding bikes and tricycles, racing to the post
box and back, bumping over the cracks in the pavement and steering past trees planted by the Council
in squares of crusty brown root-infested soil.

I wanted to stay sitting in the car at the station
forecourt but mum wouldn't let me. So we went
together to the platform. There are notices on the
inside of train doors: *Do not alight until the train
has stopped*. And that is just what the Snow Queen
did when the train stopped — she *alighted*. A blue
suitcase in each hand, a bag slung over one shoulder, she negotiated the steps without looking down.
A man held the door open for her. No doubt she
had practised deportment when she was younger,
gliding up and down the stairs with a book on her
head. Mum rushed forward to help her. I joined
them and took one of the suitcases. A tupperware
box lay at the top of her open bag: the Snow Queen

had had a packed lunch. The teaspoon with which she had eaten her yoghurt was wrapped in a plastic bag to prevent it making a mess.

Why had she come to stay?

Mum wanted to know why I had asked: *She's free to stay if she wants, isn't she, she has been to stay before, hasn't she?* But now the Snow Queen was married, and I thought everything had changed. She has visited us three years beforehand, and the age gap of seven years had made all the difference; but now I was fourteen and somehow the gap between fourteen and twenty-one was not so great. Mum had decided that the Snow Queen could have my sister Lydia's room while Lydia was away. Lydie, I knew, would not be pleased. She feels similarly to me about the Snow Queen. You could never find anyone more different from the Snow Queen than Lydie. When we were small Lydie and I would fight and she would dig her nails into me and draw blood. Louise, the Snow Queen, had no scars upon her; and each of her nails was perfectly shaped. When she stepped down from the train I saw that her blonde bob had recently been trimmed. It has been highlighted again too; and if highlighted much more, her ends would need attention. It made her look as if she was going grey. It suited her.

I noticed her legs, too, as she walked ahead of me to the car. She had what grandma terms a well-turned ankle, nothing but bone. Lydia has square calves, thick ankles, the sort of legs that accompany flat sandals. Lydia and I are not alike in that respect: I exercise my ankles every evening as I watch telly, making arcs and circles. When she was young the Snow Queen had had a party frock. I know what mum says, I know that the Snow Queen had only a

father, and that fathers don't know much about that
sort of thing, but all the same I'm sure that I would
have refused any party frocks. If she had been born
a Victorian, the Snow Queen would have been one
of those women with an eighteen-inch waist and a
pained expression. I know that she's had a sad life
and all that, but she's never made an effort to help
herself.

The Snow Queen was not suited to the summer.
In the car as we drove back along the High Street
she was paler than ever. We drove past the arcade
of shops that have been there for as long as I can
remember. The pharmacy is crammed with Max
Factor and Rimmel and Outdoor Girl, with cans
of glittery hairspray which never sell, with meal
replacement muesli bars, and jars of ginseng, and
instamatic cameras and special-offer photo albums,
comb cases and key-rings and packets of barley
sugar. Next to the pharmacy is the hosiery shop,
its window display never varying: tea-bag coloured
tights alongside reduced price blue winceyette pyjamas, short sleeved winter vests (fawn, size 16), tap-
estry cushion cover kits (ideal as gifts), and a peg bag.
We drove past the green grocers and the pram shop.
At the end of the High Street there is the Italian
Restaurant, *Il Giardino*. The lunchtime menu was
as usual chalked up outside: *Today, ravioli*. The
Snow Queen suffered from travel sickness on hot
days. Her eyes swam in a colourless face. She was
pale and moist like a lump of sweaty cheese.

But ladies glow. The Snow Queen glowed with
lines traceable like lines of down, traceable in
trickles: a line above her top lip and a trickle
across her forehead. She held a handful of tissues
soggy with cologne. I remembered that she had been

on holiday with us to Majorca six or seven years previously. Mum had persuaded Lydia and me to go without our tops as we played at the poolside, to let the air get to us. The Snow Queen sat every day in her C&A bikini on a lilo, under a shade, reading a paperback and muddying slightly the edges of each page with the suntan oil that clung to her fingers. The sun had burned white rings around her pale blue irises. It lit them like the haloes which drift around the moon before rain. She stared at us through her albino lashes like a crazed moth, luminous and about to dive-bomb a lamp bulb. Later she took to wearing black reflective glasses. Lydia and I were convinced that she shaved her legs. No one could be as hairless as she was. Now, of course, I realise that she would never have shaved. She would have used some caustic lemon-scented lotion to melt it all away.

She was having a shower. She had had a cup of tea and then she had said she would like to freshen up. I had gone into the garden to catch the last of the sun. Everything was in shade except the rockery. I sat on a flat stone, facing the house. Mum was in the kitchen, at the window, drying the tea cups and replacing them in the cupboard. I could see her as she turned in the darkness between the sink and the shelves; the tea towel flickering, a broad strip of white linen. She bowed her head and wiped the inside of each cup with a sharp twist of her wrist. I could hear the shower. Water rose as thick hot steam through an open window, and splashed from drainpipe to drain near the back door. A ball of froth collected in the grid like a snowball. Why had Lydie

left me to the Snow Queen? She had gone away for
a week to stay with a friend. Perhaps that was why
the Snow Queen had decided to visit. But, then, I
doubt whether she had known; and I doubt whether
she had cared. She might not have liked Lydia but
she couldn't have liked me much more and I was
still around. I had planned to have the weekend to
myself; me and mum on our own around the house,
taking the radio into the garden, dragging the sun
lounger from the shed, and making plates of cottage
cheese salad for lunch.

She is mum's daughter, not dad's. Mum had been
married before and when she left her husband and
went home to grandma the little Ice Maiden stayed
behind with her father. They stayed up north somewhere. I suppose it was her home. We had visited
them for the Snow Queen's wedding. She had been
saving up, working in a bank. All girls who work in
banks are engaged — solitaire diamond on the third
finger, left hand — and have cheap mortgages. At
her wedding the Snow Queen was dressed in white.
She had enlisted the help of a local dressmaker to
sew her in, tuck her up and hand-finish her in good
time: the individual touch. She had booked a choir
too. Lydia almost laughed herself sick at the reception because I said it was a shame that the Snow
Queen had removed her veil for the photos. Mum
overheard us and then avoided us all afternoon, being polite instead to ancestors and handing around
plates of those stubby sausages speared with sticks.
The Snow Queen's husband, Mike, was nothing
special. At the reception he spent the first hour or so
cavorting around the tableclothed trestle tables with
his Rugby Club chums, lobbing pineapple cubes
and clenching carnations between his teeth. Later

he looked flushed, his starched shirt stretched at
the seams. He adopted a manner like that of a
schoolboy at his father's funeral, humbly accept-
ing responsibility and bursting with pride. Towards
the end of the afternoon he lurched alone between
tables cleared of everything but the currants and
crumbs of icing dropped from the cake.

I sat in the garden and wondered how much
longer the Snow Queen would stay in the bathroom.
At the start of each visit she would line her potions
along the window sill: conditioner with real silk;
squeezy tubes and screw-top jars and a clear plastic
toothbrush; unperfumed baby soap in a dish in a
washbag. The little things annoyed me — why did
she have to bring her own handcream? Why not use
ours, kept in the cabinet? But she brought her own,
*pour peau sec*; but no Dead Sea Mud face pack, and
no hair gel. She had a modest array of trial samples
and Boot's own, all pine-leaf lotion-green coloured.
I sat in the garden and listened to the tinkling of a
distant piano: next door Mrs Trayherne was at her
evening practice.

When the sun had disappeared from the rockery I
went upstairs to my bedroom. I lay on my bed thinking how I'd like a bath, a cool clear bath: to lie in
the water and trace the pattern in the tiles, the white
wisps in the blue; and there was the shower curtain
sweeping to the floor, thick flaccid plastic printed
with grasses and butterflies; and mum's shower cap
hanging frilly on a plastic hook. Before going to the
bathroom the Snow Queen had spoken on the phone
to her husband. We had been sitting downstairs at
the kitchen table when the phone had rung. The
Snow Queen had sipped tea, her legs crossed, her
feet slipped into neat new olive-green Marks and

Spencer shoes. I had gone into the hall to answer the phone because I had expected it to be for me. But it wasn't.

'It's Michael,' I called.

I had waited and dropped the receiver into her hand when she arrived. She had inclined her head, hair swinging, and placed the receiver to her ear.

'Hello?'

I waited a long time in my bedroom; how was I to have known that she was still in the bathroom? There are no locks on any of the doors in this house — we sing — so I had pushed open the bathroom door, and there she was: fully clothed, sitting on the edge of the bath, bent double; her feet in green shoes spread across the tiles; her hands clenched bloodless over the enamel rim; her eyes burning with tears.

Downstairs mum stood at a work surface in her apron, dicing a carrot, cutting into the chopping board. I sat on a stool, picking up the *TV Times* and flicking through the pages.

'What's wrong with Louise?' I asked her.

'Nothing that need concern you,' she replied.

She finished slicing and I reached over and took a piece. She swept the rest into her hand and dropped them into a colander.

'I'll be upstairs,' I said, 'in my room.'

I bit into the carrot and got down from the stool. I crossed the room and stopped at the door for a second.

'I'll be listening to records,' I said. 'I'll be down in time for tea.'

# AN OUTER
# LONDON CHILDHOOD

'You think you're above the law, don't you,' my mother
would say.

'Not above the law,' I'd taunt in reply, 'but below
it; below it and waiting for it to swoop.'

Then she would sigh and purse her lips and say it
was my age and that she had never brought me up
to be like this. It was something she said whenever
I skipped school or cheated fares or bought clothes
from Marks and Spencer's to wear before returning them for a refund. But she never objected to
my great-grandmother leaving restaurants without
paying the bill. On these occasions my great-
grandmother chose a table by the door to enable
a quick getaway. My mother thought it hilarious.

My mother had invited me to her fiftieth birthday
party; for family and friends, she said, although she
usually claimed to have neither. So I had travelled
from Clapham, where I had lived for the past four
years, to spend the afternoon at my parents' home in
Essex. I had travelled from Liverpool Street Station
by train, and paid the full fare. My mother hates
me to cheat the fare: 'Don't evade the fare,' she
would beg, impressed by posters of fare dodgers

losing their jobs as bank managers. Throughout the journey Essex appeared to have been above water but appearances were deceptive: I stepped from the train and sank into mud. There was a cold wind and I regretted having chosen to wear a skirt. The platform was deserted, so after the train had departed I left the platform without relinquishing my ticket and crossed the tracks towards the house.

When I entered the house my mother was at the table eating vol au vents, circled by people holding paper plates and telling her how well she looked.

'Fat, you mean,' she replied to each. She picked the prawn from the top of each vol au vent and ate it. When I was a child she had licked her plate at the end of each meal; my father had objected.

'Waste not want not,' she had giggled in reply.

I had been terrified that she would do it when my friends came to tea; or, worse, that she would sit naked in the garden. She used to like to sit naked in the sun while shaving her legs and telling me how she belonged in the jungle with a bone through her nose. She used to cry whenever it rained and in the summer she wore miniskirts in colours of cough mixture and penicillin syrup. Every evening in the living room she danced on her own to Jackson Five records, and she bought an afro wig to wear at parties.

But now she was fifty; she no longer wore miniskirts and she had never worn the afro wig which had been claimed by us for the dressing-up basket. For the party she wore a dress chosen for her by my father. She caught sight of me and called to me across the room.

'Vegetarian,' she shouted, lifting a plate of prawnless vol au vents.

She turned to the guests who had gathered around

her. 'Vegetarian,' she confided to them, 'my daughter is a vegetarian.'

They murmured appreciatively and said to each other that they didn't eat much red meat themselves these days.

My mother joined their conversation with enthusiasm. 'We never did eat much red meat,' she claimed triumphantly, 'because we couldn't afford it.'

But I remembered roast on Sundays and mince on Monday. I sidled close to her and whispered in her ear: 'Boiled bacon.'

She turned to face me. 'Don't start,' she hissed, 'don't start: we had boiled bacon once in a blue moon and you know it.'

'Pease pudding?'

There was silence, and she smiled briefly at her guests before turning again to me. 'You're being unfair,' she protested to me, 'and now you're going to say that I brought you up all wrong.'

But I remembered that I had been brought up well: I had been given tea, toast and cereal for breakfast each morning; and there had been two slices of toast, one with marmite and one with honey. I had been given the marmite first and then the honey — savoury things first, then sweet — but had often been unhappy about this: 'Why not the honey first?' I had protested.

My mother had sighed on these occasions and turned to me with her lips pursed and said, 'Just do as I say.'

I moved with my mother from the table to the window. We watched my sister Catherine arrive.

'Larger than life,' my mother remarked to me.

We watched Catherine hurl the car door shut, bracelets and bangles colliding on her arm. We watched as she glanced at her watch and tugged at her blouse and advanced towards the house; her stilettos rapping the pavement; a fiancé behind her. The fiancé carried parcels wrapped in coloured foil and topped with rosettes. We listened as someone opened the front door. Catherine loomed by the window and we overheard the greetings. Within seconds she was in the living room, trotting among grandmothers and aunties and smearing them with kisses.

My mother turned to me. 'Look at her posture,' she whispered, 'she'll have trouble when it comes to childbearing.'

Catherine was swathed in crêpe de chine, tucked and seamed: Catalogue Classic. Headlines insisted at the start of the summer that shorter skirts would be fashionable; but Catherine, unfortunately, has square knees.

My mother moved behind me. 'You ought to say hello to her,' she said.

I protested: 'She's horrible.'

'Yes, but she's your sister.' My mother stood firm. 'You ought to make an effort.'

Catherine, however, had already seen us. She stopped in the middle of the room, flanked by aunties. 'Hello mum,' she said, her teeth shiny, 'you're looking well.'

'So are you,' replied my mother hastily, 'so are you.'

The aunties gathered around Catherine and asked her about her job, flat, car, and fiancé. They asked

me what I was up to, and what I was doing with
myself.

'This and that,' I told them.

'Still painting?'

Swimming, mostly: I wondered whether they had
noticed that I smelled of chlorine. I had a blue plastic leisure pass: for the unemployed, permitting me
to swim at reduced charge during off-peak hours. I
swam twenty or thirty lengths every day. I had always liked swimming. I had lessons, weekly, when
I was a child: I had taken tests — bronze, silver and
gold Personal Survival Awards — treading water
wearing old pyjamas. I had had riding lessons too;
and ballet, and tap. The dance classes had taken
place on Saturday mornings at the Jean Wilson
School of Ballet in the High Street. There had been
a show every Christmas with printed programmes
sponsored by the florist and the butcher. I had passed the exams — Royal School of Ballet, preliminary
and elementary, grade one and grade two — with
pink silk ribbon wound around my ankles. I had
hated school sports; I had hated navy blue knickers
and mid-winter hockey games.

'You're not sporty,' my mother had explained, 'because you're academic.'

'But Catherine's neither.'

My brother was considered artistic by my mother
because of his asthma.

My mother had wanted lots of children: she had
wanted to sit in a rocking chair on a verandah with
grandchildren at her feet. She had wanted five children but she has four and I am the eldest. I had
been born when she was twenty-five. My parents
had been saving for a home of their own and living
in the meantime in my grandmother's attic.

'The attic,' my brother would remind us during the rows around the kitchen table on Sunday lunchtimes, 'with no water and no heating.'

'The attic,' my mother would interject, 'which smelled of cabbage. The attic for which I paid rent.' At this point she would lean across the table and jab at him with her fork. 'And I paid my mother for my Sunday lunch too.'

He would then push his plate close to the cruet to display to us his portion of Yorkshire pudding: a lump of sweet-smelling fat crusted upon his gravy.

'I bet your portions were bigger than mine.'

My mother would purse her lips before replying: 'They weren't, as a matter of fact.'

I had been born when my parents were twenty-five: they had bought a home of their own and my mother had commuted to work for six months, retching during each journey with morning sickness. She left work when I was born. The births of Catherine, Luke and Clare followed at four-yearly intervals. She considered naming her last baby Gloria but decided against it on the grounds that it was a barmaid's name. She once told my brother that she had thought of naming him Zebedee; and he replied with disgust that he would have left home. She laughed at him and told us that it was the only mistake she had ever made.

Clare had been born when I was twelve. By that time I had endured a year of Mr Newman's biology classes and learned that when a man and woman love each other the penis becomes erect. No one else in my class had a pregnant mother. No one else had a mother who was a pacifist and an atheist. Our history teacher, Miss Tribe, asked us to discover what our parents thought of Winston Churchill and my mother told me that he was a silly old git. She said the same of the vicar despite the allegations that he had said unorthodox things in confirmation classes. She claimed that I attended a Church of England school because of the good teacher-pupil ratio. She had been obsessively interested in my education and had continued to write to my French penfriends long after I had stopped. She had read all the historical fiction in the local library, and it was she who told me that Anne of Cleves had smelled.

My father cannot believe that I am not a stock-broker. During the Sunday lunchtime rows, whilst splattering trifle into his bowl, he would tell me how he wished that he'd had half the opportunities I had.

'You should work your way up,' he would conclude.

'Up what?' I'd ask.

'Or you should travel.'

I pointed out to him on these occasions that travel necessitates return. When I left home he told me that a girl could do worse than learn to type. My mother agreed: 'It stands you in good stead.' At school she had passed the eleven plus whereas he had failed it. Then she had passed five 'O' levels and left school for a job in an office because her mother had needed her wages. She had wanted me to study hard and find a good job, but I studied too hard and ended up at University. And students, according to my parents, took drugs.

'Drugs,' I'd say, reaching across the table for the milk, 'like tea or coffee perhaps?'

They told me on these occasions not to be clever. My mother's cousin had been clever: he had been a student, and had visited us one Sunday afternoon with his father and been rude throughout *Bridge*

*Over the River Kwai*. My mother remarked to me after they had left that she didn't like war films either but that his rudeness had been quite unnecessary.

My father disapproved of sex before marriage, and once he told me so while sitting at the kitchen table reading the newspaper. Catherine and Luke had left for work and my mother was accompanying Clare to school.

'I'll never marry,' I told him.

He turned a page. 'All normal people marry,' he said.

'Nowadays they usually marry twice,' I said.

He glanced at me.

'Which must create problems,' I continued, spooning jam onto my toast, 'at Hallowe'en, when a young girl is supposed to light a candle and stand at a mirror to catch a glimpse of her future husband. What do you suppose she sees these days? Two of them, vying for position, pushing and shoving in the background?'

His mouth had dried into a line. He closed the newspaper, placed it on the table, and rose.

'Don't push me, child,' he said, 'because I'm nasty when I'm angry.'

The following day he informed Catherine of his beliefs.

'Crap,' she said slicing bread for sandwiches, 'because you and mum went on holiday together before you were married, and I know because I've seen the photos, and you can't tell me you had single beds.'

It had been my parents' first holiday together: they have photographs of each other at Lands End, smiling and pointing out at sea.

'It's true,' my mother said. She was kneeling at the fridge, searching each shelf for cheese. She told us that whilst he made the booking she had stayed in the car. I remembered my parents' first car from the photographs: large and black and shiny like something in an Ealing comedy.

'He booked single rooms,' she told us, 'and I cried when he told me.'

She found the lump of cheese and took it from the fridge. She closed the door and turned towards my father.

'You're a hypocrite,' she said, unwrapping the cheese, 'because you don't believe in sex before marriage for your daughters, but for Luke things are different.'

'Luke's a boy,' my father replied.

'I suspected as much,' she said, 'from the pin-ups on his wall and the pornography under his bed; I suspected something was wrong.'

Luke had been fourteen when his ex-girlfriend had called at our house claiming to be pregnant. I had not been at home at the time and I was told about it later. My mother related with sympathy that the girl had been carrying a cushion under her jumper. Clare confirmed that the cushion had been square and edged with tassles.

My mother's story of the cushion was a favourite of mine; and another was how she had been conceived before her parents' wedding. She had discovered that she had been born a healthy baby six months after the wedding.

'It can't be true!' I'd protest, delighted.

'It's true,' she'd confirm with a smile.

But surely it could not be true of my mother's mother: not grandma, who wore a pinney and collected blue and white china and played *Come Back to Sorrento* on the piano; not grandma, with her milky puddings and the touch of cold cream around her eyes before bedtime; not grandma, surely? During the war my grandmother had stayed in London when my mother was evacuated to relatives who dressed her in a liberty bodice and forbade games on Sundays. My grandmother joined her one Christmas with a new baby born deaf and blind and dying. My mother returned after the war, crawling under the dining table and staying there for days, her father a stranger across the parlour telling her stories.

The stories of my mother's London childhood are of attics and cellars and lodgers, of London schools with stone playgrounds and steep staircases and high windows, and of peasoupers and trams. My own memories of London are, however, of the Science Museum: of the simulated rocket launches and of the icecream vans that lined the roads outside. The icecream was squirted into cones and laced with red sauce.

'No 99s,' my mother decreed whenever she bought me a cone, 'because they're expensive and the flake is unnecessary.'

I have memories of other day trips: I remember the Ideal Home Exhibition, the journey on the train from Cockfosters (cheap day returns, one and a half), and the gadgets and samples, the new type of cheese grater or the wind chimes for my bedroom or the bag full of leaflets about formica kitchens.

When I was a child there was a box of my mother's things in the loft: ballet shoes and a school scarf; ice skating boots and a vanity case. On wintry Sundays I climbed into the loft and sat bedside it, close to the water tank, and explored the folds of tissue paper.

There were exercise books with royal blue covers, feint ruled, containing English and French, Biology and Geography; and sketch books, four of them, full of sketches. There was a photograph, too, of my mother with two friends in a park: young women in skimpy cardigans, laughing, their arms around one another's shoulders. She worked at that time in an office in the city; the women were workmates. Then she met my father: he worked in the basement as an apprentice among the printing presses. They met every evening after dark on the steps of St Paul's, sheltering under my mother's umbrella and telling each other the stories of their future. She once wore fake tan but it ran in streaks down her legs in the rain.

It rained at their wedding, and the photographs are of bride and groom sheltering in the church porch. My father had wanted a church wedding so they married at a church in his home town: High Anglican, in the High Street. He lived in the countryside, twenty miles from London, and this had impressed my mother. She had wanted to leave London ever since her return after the war; so after saving the earnings from their weekday jobs, their evening jobs and jobs at weekends, they packed their things in boxes lined with tissue paper and left the attic for a home of their own in Essex. They ceased commuting when I was born: my father rented space in a pre-fab office behind the railway station and my mother did the bookwork on the kitchen table at home.

My mother visited the doctor when I was two years old: she was afraid of gaining weight. He swivelled in his chair, the stethoscope dangling around his neck, and told her that she was not fat.

'No,' she told me later, 'but *he* was.'

He had a drink problem, and his patients knew about it: his wife had retired as Brown Owl because of family problems. His patients blamed him for their illnesses and for the deaths of their relatives. No one ever chose to consult him and the reception-ist had to claim that there were no other doctors available. He was right, of course, about my mother not being fat: she was by that time emaciated. She was afraid not only of fatness but of germs and planes. Whenever she heard planes she ran indoors and hid under the table. The doctor's advice to her was that she should ask someone to slap her around the face with a wet fish, and that she should have another baby.

Her second pregnancy was difficult, her blood pressure rose, and she was admitted to hospital for a rest. After a month in hospital she took a lift to the fourth floor hairdressing salon and threat-ened to jump. She was then allowed home to rest. Catherine was a difficult baby: despite the bows in her hair she was burly and aggressive; she was too fat to crawl but dragged herself screaming to her feet and gripped and shook the bars of her play-pen. When she was six months old my parents went abroad alone for a fortnight, driving across Spain in the family car and sending us postcards of dancers with frilly dresses. Catherine and I stayed at home with grandma, who made for my packed lunch each day a round of sandwiches: white bread spread with lemon curd or honey, folded, wrapped, and laid in a tupperware box. My mother had insisted that I have three rounds: one of meat and two of cheese (one with pickle and one without), along with a yoghurt, a banana, and a chocolate biscuit. When I returned home from school each day grandma was sitting at the kitchen table in a housecoat of light blue cotton and polyester, or pink perhaps, or gingham, with the sleeves rolled up; her elbow on the table, her chin resting in her hand. She read magazines, flicking through pages of knit-one-purl-one Stylish Summer Tops, or of Summer Fayre fruit fool and cheesecakes and date bars with a crunchy nut topping.

Luke had been a lovely baby, my mother claimed, although she had not wanted a boy.

'A boy at last,' the consultant had said to her during the ward round: so she spat at him. She waited four years after the birth of Luke until deciding to have a fourth child. I had wanted a pony. My father insisted that we could have one or the other but not both. My mother won; but then the doctor wanted to know why she had not been happy with three children, and told her that the current population explosion was a serious threat to mankind; and other people wanted to know if the pregnancy had been a mistake, because after all she was nearly forty. She replied on each occasion that the baby had been planned. My father, when he said anything about it at all, claimed otherwise; and then my mother would cross her hands over her stomach and raise her eyes to the ceiling and exclaim that it took two to tango. She gained weight and laughed and patted her stomach, wondering aloud about the possibility of twins. But every night I heard her in the hallway upstairs at the airing cupboard folding towels and crying.

Family photographs have always been taken by my father. At my mother's fiftieth birthday party he waved at me from across the room. 'Out of the way!' he shouted, aiming the camera at my mother. Then he turned his attention to the guests.

'Smile, please, ladies,' he requested, flourishing the camera. He shouted at his grandmother to smile but she did not hear him and continued to nod instead at those whom she considered to be admiring her hat. She had admitted to my mother that it had been stolen from Selfridges. The guests were gathering around the table to admire my mother's presents. I remembered birthdays and Christmases, the wrapping paper rustling in my mother's room each night; the lamplight dimmed behind her door. The guests had begun to call for her to cut the cake.

Birthday girl, they called her.

She turned towards me, the curtain catching on a link in her watchstrap.

'I can't,' she whispered, 'I can't; I don't want to. To tell you the truth, I don't want to do much these days. Is it my age?'

I reached for her wrist and disengaged it from the curtain.

'No,' I said, 'I don't think so.'

There is a photograph in the album in which she is not yet disengaged from the curtain, and her lips are parted but silent; but this is not how I remember her. Before leaving the party I made my excuses to the aunties and then spoke with her again. She had been eating the last of the vol au vents.

'A shame to waste them,' she explained as I approached her.

'Mother,' I said, 'I have a place at Art College.'

She licked her forefinger and ran it around the

empty plate before licking it again. 'Art College,' she mused. 'How nice.'

'But three more years of study,' I reminded her.

She reached across the table to stack plates.

'So I don't know what to do,' I said.

She shrugged. I handed her an empty plate.

'So what shall I do?' I asked. I reached for her and laid my hand over hers. She laid the pile of plates on the table and turned towards me with a frown.

She sighed. 'Well I wouldn't give it up,' she said with a shrug. 'Not now,' she said, more definitely, 'not if I were you.'